The Ease of Time

Charlotte Rowan

spectrum books

To Theo, for giving me the push I needed to keep going.

Chapter One

"London is an absolute travesty. I can't believe we have to queue for two hours to see a possibly really bland exhibit."

"If you had been on time, we wouldn't have to wait," Katie answers, obviously still annoyed.

"And I apologised for that," I reply. "Many times. But excuse me if spending an afternoon looking at paintings of straight white couples doesn't fill me with impatience."

"It doesn't matter that they're straight or white or anything. What matters is that they love each other. Those paintings celebrate that."

"Yeah, sure," I say, as if to compromise.

Except I can't keep my mouth shut.

"But don't tell me you actually think the women in those paintings were really in love with their husbands."

I point at the program.

"Most of the art dates back to the 18th and 19th century. Cows had nearly more value than women back then. I doubt love was a major component of marriages."

"Do you have to be so cynical all the time?" Katie whispers angrily.

She looks around as if I was shaming her in front of the other suckers willing to go see that exhibition. I roll my eyes in answer.

"I just thought…" she starts, now gazing at me almost hopefully.

Her range of expressions never ceases to astonish me.

"I just thought it could be... romantic?"

I wince at that.

"Our definition must differ, then. For me, romanticism implies meaningful acts that also happen to be useful. Whereas for you, it seems to be: 'Let's waste an afternoon looking at lame paintings of boring people'. You can't blame me for being a little uninterested."

She turns her back to me, now properly angry, and I'm not sure I actually mind. The queue moves on slowly and eventually—after an inappropriate amount of time spent in silence—we're in. And it's... Yeah. It's terrible.

"It's boring," I say, in case my expression isn't clear enough.

"We literally just arrived."

"And it's literally not interesting."

"Maybe if you stopped being such a bitch and actually looked at the art, you could find it interesting," Katie snaps.

"And where would be the fun in that?"

Mumbling, I follow her along the gallery, trying not to think too hard about what else I could be doing. Sadly enough, there's so, so much. When I let out a sad sigh at the thought, Katie turns to me sharply.

"What now?"

"Can you please chill?"

"How am I supposed to do that when you're being a child?"

"Oh, I'm sorry to be expressing my discomfort by sighing in your proximity."

"For once, we're doing something I want to do and you have to ruin it!" she whispers, her voice strained, tears already in her eyes.

"Oh please, don't start crying again."

"Don't tell me what to do!"

"You just told me not to sigh?"

"Stop being flippant!"

I stare at her expressively. That's enough to make her stomp away towards more of the outdated paintings. I sigh once more, with feelings. I know I shouldn't push her, but everything has just been bad lately. Well, not everything. Most things are fine, at best. But Katie and I...

I shake my head, trying to dislodge the thought that comes back too often these days. I'm sure I felt something special for her when we met. But now, it's like we're stuck in the awkward relationship of casual lovers with not much in common, who stay together mostly because the loneliness would be too much to bear otherwise.

I see her blue jumper in the corner of my eye, further down in the room, her back resolutely to me. Making my way to the opposite end of the gallery, I spot an empty corner with a couch and decide to just sit until she's ready to go. Then, we'll head back to mine, and we'll fight, and we'll kiss, and it will all be fine again for a few weeks until... Until.

Even the couch is awful, which is not that surprising for a newly opened gallery that doesn't offer free alcohol. They could at least do something about the quality of the seats. I take out my phone to kill time, but quickly put it back in my bag after a quick scroll revealing photos of babies, too-perfect-to-be-sincere weddings, house renovations and joyous family reunions. I wish I was smart enough to simply delete all these apps, but sadly, my self-destructive side is stronger.

The possibility of simply leaving the gallery grazes my mind. Yes, Katie would be furious and vexed, but maybe that would be for the best. She never really said it clearly, but I know she wants more from me. She wants everything I just saw on the app; she wants the life partner, the kids, the house. The idea of it repulses me. Why should I want something I never needed?

At this stage of my train of my thought, I should remind myself that I don't want all of this because I want more from my life, because I'm not ready to give up on everything I planned for myself. But when I think of goals, of dreams, of expectations, there's nothing but a big gaping void expanding by the day. So yeah, maybe I should just leave. Maybe it would just be easier...

Feeling suddenly exhausted, I close my eyes and rest my head against the wall, narrowly avoiding the bottom of the frame that's hung on it. Twisting my neck, I catch a lateral view of soft shapes and colours, and I'm intrigued enough to get up to look more closely, taking a few steps back. This one is... not bland. While imperfect, it's actually quite good, I realise, as I squint to study it better.

First of all, two women are represented which, hopefully, means some sapphic action. That would be a good surprise. But it's not the only thing that sets it apart from the rest. The colours that seemed pale from where I was sitting are anything but. The shades of the faces are bright and natural. The folds of the dresses, the flying strands of hair seem so real that I can almost feel their texture under my fingers.

The woman in the centre is sitting on an ornamented chair, her back straight, her eyes almost defiant. The corners of her lips are raised slightly in a teasing smile. Her brown hair is piled up in a clean bun, some curled strands kissing her forehead and ears. Her lips coloured with a blush of light pink seem to call to me, and the forest green shade of her dress is complimented by a simple pearl necklace highlighting her slim neck.

One of her hands rests close to her head on the chair's back, the tips of her fingers nearly meeting the hand of her possible partner, who's standing up. This second woman has shorter hair that is vaguely held by a lace, strands hiding most of her face, but not enough to erase the look of tenderness and, I guess, love she sets on the other woman. Her lips are shaping a smile that feels somewhat familiar.

The longer I stare at the painting, the more this feeling grows. My lips curve against my understanding, emotions from the painting encircling me. It feels like the eyes of the first woman are following me, as if she knew me. As if she had been expecting me...

A sudden gulf of air brushes my ear, and I hear my name whispered in a chorus of voices, the sound drifting all around. As I look for its origin, the people walking in the gallery begin to feel further than before, less present.

Turning to the painting once more, a detail catches my eye. There, just under the standing woman's sleeve, dark lines entwine, covering her wrist. My eyes fall on my own arm, the black curves of my tattoos clearer than ever, identical lines appearing below the rolled-up cuff of my shirt.

I start to step back, but stop, startled and confused. Inexplicably, I find myself walking *towards* the painting, my boots quiet on the floor. The first woman's expression seems to shift, curiosity mixing to the amusement and brightening her features as her hand settles on the second woman's, their fingers now entwined.

Entranced, I raise my own hand, fingers stretched towards theirs, so close and—

Chapter Two

The first thing I notice when I come to are the smells, strong and all-consuming, reviving my nose used to car fumes and stale underground air. Then, the silence. The colours, bright and clean.

I roll on my back where I apparently fell, wondering how and when I left the gallery to end up in a vast field. A question immediately followed by how did I happen to find such a large field in East London... I look for landmarks, something I recognise from the Hackney marshes maybe, but there's nothing except grass and trees on the horizon, a few cows lounging lazily a little further away.

Whatever is happening, I don't plan on hanging around to find out. So I try to get up, but as soon as my left feet touches the ground, a pinching pain crawls up my leg, making me groan. I shake my ankle a little, the pain aggravating.

Then, a gasp.

I look around frantically, searching for the person responsible, and relax a little when my gaze falls on a child in an oversize dress who's staring up at me, bemusement written all over her face.

"Who are you?" she asks, a curious inflexion in her voice.

"Who are *you*?" I shoot back.

I look around at the empty field.

"Where are your parents? You probably shouldn't be roaming around on your own in the middle of nowhere?"

The kid doesn't answer, only staring at me some more. I wrench a hand through my hair with a sigh and move to kneel in front of her, trying to muster the patience I need to talk to a child while lost somewhere in the countryside.

"Okay, kid, work with me here. Where do you live? Is there someone you could call? Also... where are we?"

Patting my jeans to localize my phone, I realise with a curse that it must be in my backpack, which apparently did not make the trip with me. I look at the kid, who seems to be around 10 or 12 maybe, and wonder if that's old enough to have a phone. Probably yes. Especially if they are left to wander around on their own.

"Do you have a phone I could borrow? We should call your parents. Also, Maps would be super helpful right now."

She squints at me.

"You appear to be quite strange," are her next words.

And while I pride myself on being a little queer in every sense of the word, it's not the encouragement I need at this moment.

"Quite. But how about you help me out a little, anyway?"

I take her lack of answer for a form of willingness and press on.

"First, again, who are you? Second, and most importantly, where am I?"

"My name is Alice. And over there is Allander House. My home," she says, pointing vaguely above her shoulder.

Straining my eyes, I think I can discern a glimpse of red tile between two thick trees.

"Right, your home... Which is where?"

"There," she says, pointing again in the same direction and looking at me as if I was stupid.

A good reminder why I dislike kids. As I start to hop towards the tree line, desperate to find someone more helpful, she steps in front of me.

"Mamma will not like your clothes. How come you are dressed in this manner?"

"That's about the least of my problems, what your mum thinks," I mutter, ignoring her question and walking past her.

She doesn't have to hurry much to match my pace.

"And what are those on your arms?" she asks, pointing at where my sleeves are rolled up. "What a strange idea it is to draw on one's skin... But I believe I have seen such marks in the library, in those books where—"

She interrupts herself.

"What books?" I ask reluctantly when I notice her frown.

"Stories of travel in civilisations far away. I read that warriors sometimes get marks on their skin to prove their courage. I did not know it was also possible for women, however..."

"Women can do all that men can and more," I say distractedly, trying to ignore the pain that ignites in my ankle when I swerve to avoid a puddle. "Maybe you should change the sort of books you read if they make you think like that."

When Alice slows down to glare at me, I sigh and turn to her.

"I think you are quite mean," she remarks.

"I think you are quite right."

But for some reason, looking at her vexed expression makes me feel guilty. And tired. So, so tired.

"Look... Alice. I don't know why I'm here or how I got here. Maybe, for some reason, I went on a bender and don't remember a thing, but honestly, I just want to go back. I'm not trying to be mean,

I'm just trying to not be lost. So please, *please*, could you help me out a little?"

She seems to think for a moment, but then, thanks to the wonders of innocence, she takes my hand and leads me towards the trees. As we leave the sun behind us, a voice rings.

"Alice! Come here this instant!"

The kid immediately drops my hand and runs to a young woman in an old-timey dress approaching quickly, staring hard at me. Her expression somewhat softens when she gets close enough.

"My apologies," she says. "I thought you were a man!"

"Assuming someone's gender is rude," I mumble under my breath.

"Pardon me?"

"Nothing..."

"She does that a lot," Alice chimes in. "Speaking nonsense in a low voice and frowning."

She follows with what, I assume, she believes to be a good imitation of me, eyebrows crunched to her nose and mouth in a straight line.

"I don't look like that!" I object, looking exactly like that.

The two faces answering me leave no doubt about it.

"Whatever, I'm allowed to, it's been a long day," I complain. "So, could you please tell me *exactly* where I am?"

"Near our home," the woman says, pointing in the same vague direction the kid did earlier.

I pinch the top of my nose.

"Yes, I understood that. But where is that? Walthamstow? Please don't say Leyton..."

"Pardon? Do you mean Mitcham? But it is further north from here..."

Her confusion is quickly replaced by worry.

"Are you lost? And oh, dear God, you are hurt," she exclaims, pointing at my left leg on which I'm clearly trying not to rest. "Whatever should we do?"

She looks at me, then at Alice, as if we had all the answers. The thrumming pain in my ankle does not help me focus. It takes me a second too long to register her words.

"Wait, what do you mean Mitcham? Where even *is* Mitcham?"

"I am not quite sure I understand," the woman hesitates, more confused than ever.

Sitting down dramatically, head in my hands, I think hard to try and understand what the hell is going on. But as I scramble to put together the pieces of this peculiar puzzle, none seem to match.

Unless...

I study the cut of their dresses, their flat shoes, the way the young woman's hair is carefully tied in a crown around her head. And there are the words they use, the tone of their sentences...

"Hey," I say, my voice heavy with dread. "What... What year is it?"

The woman stares at me for a moment, visibly puzzled and concerned.

"Did you also happen to hurt your head? Should we call for the doctor? Perhaps—"

"Just. Answer the question. Please," I insist, adding pressure on my temples to fight the incoming headache.

"Well... Today is May the 29th, in the year 1813."

Shocked, I freeze, looking for a trace of denial on her face. I find none.

So I do the next logical thing.

I pass out.

Chapter Three

I wake up with a headache threatening to burst my head open. As the pain behind my eyes begins to subside, I look around carefully, taking in my surroundings.

My very unfamiliar surroundings.

I'm not sure what time it is because heavy curtains are covering the windows, blocking the outside. There's a pile of folded clothes set at the end of the bed, on what seems to be a dark wooden chest, and a few drawings and watercolours hanging on the wall. I barely recognise myself in the mirror of the large dresser facing the bed, buried under crumpled white sheets, my hair a mess, my face too pale.

Then, my eyes find my own clothes, folded on a chair by the window. A strange feeling of dissociation takes over me as I see my jeans, shirt, and heavy boots in such an outdated decor. Confused as to what I'm wearing if my clothes are over there, I raise the cover a little and find myself in a frilly nightdress so ridiculous that I can't help but chuckle.

When I hear a noise coming from somewhere in the house, I sit up in bed, trying to focus, the events slowly coming back to me.

I fainted. I got to this strange place and fainted and am nowhere closer to understand what happened. Then I remember the reason why I fainted and drop back into bed.

1813. Somehow, I am in 1813.

That sort of thing doesn't happen. I must be high. Or dreaming. Or dead? I can't see a reason why I would have died unless something happened at the gallery...

I let out a gasp, sitting up once more.

The gallery. Katie. She's going to freak out when she realises I disappeared. What am I going to say? *"Sorry love, I got sucked into the past and ended up in my grandmother's mother's nightdress"*? Like hell she's going to believe me.

Shaking my head roughly, I try to clear my thoughts. I should probably focus on how to get back first. Right. So. I take a deep breath. This sort of thing happens all the time in books. I know books, I read books. I can sort this out.

I get up as quietly as possible, pacing around the room, examining the walls up close. In such stories, there's usually a magical gate, something the main character uses to cross back. That or magical powers, but as far as I know, I never made anything explode with my mind or a magic wand, so.

I start patting the walls, the hem of my horrifying outfit brushing against my legs at each step, and bring my ear close to listen for any hollow space. Nothing.

It takes me an undetermined amount of time to go through the room, then I start hunting for a hint, anything that could tell me why and how I'm here. But except a few boring letters and way too many ribbons for a single person, I find nothing. Almost as if the room had been emptied...

The lack of a personal touch, of a trace that anyone uses this room, makes me tick. Is it always unoccupied or was it stripped down because of me? The latter could mean whoever lives here doesn't trust me. Or is scared of me...

Remembering the look on the young woman's face when she saw me with the kid, I feel a little guilty to have been borderline rude to her. And to have fainted immediately after. But well, she told me I went back in time, so I guess she deserved it. A little.

My search resulting in nothing, I sit on the bed to gather my thoughts. I am not going at this the right way. I'm trying to rush into finding out what's happening without thinking back on what happened.

So I do.

I can remember getting to the gallery with Katie, annoying her and splitting inside. I remember sitting down and...

That painting.

The two women, their hands joined. Those lines under the dress sleeve. I look down at my own wrist, arranging the sleeve just right to see the same pattern appear. The lines of my tattoo.

It was me on that painting. It was me standing next to this woman, smiling at her with sincere affection.

I find it hard to breathe for a minute, struggling with that realization. It makes no sense, but then, so does me being here. She must be the reason why I'm here. She must also be my way back.

Problem is though... Who is she?

Chapter Four

I immediately wince as the stairs creak under my weight, my twisted ankle not helping. Pausing for a second too long, I listen for any noise betraying that someone is going to jump in front of me and ask what the hell I'm doing here.

When no one does, I gather the little courage I have left and climb down until I reach an empty, darkened corridor. Looking on both sides, I'm unsure where to go. I can see the faint shape of a door on the left which could be the front door. But while the urge to run away is tempting, I don't see how it would improve my situation. So I head right, step by step, one hand on the wall to keep my balance on the slightly uneven floor.

Soon after, I hear a melodic hum, and there, at the turn of the corridor, a faint light appears through a doorway. A rich and salty smell floats to me, making my stomach growl.

I crouch by the door, leaning just enough to see inside with one eye. It seems to be a kitchen, a guess soon confirmed by the woman I spot crossing the room in a drab brown dress and a stained apron. She's carrying a large pot, whistling softly, a relaxed expression on her face.

That changes when I lose balance. I fall lamely on my side with a curse, which is followed by a heavy thud and a shrill cry. When I finally dare to look up, the woman is backed up against the kitchen counter, stew spilled at her feet, staring at me with wide eyes.

"W–Why are you here?" she stammers.

"On the floor, or more generally?" I attempt to joke.

"The mistress said she locked the door so I needn't be frightened!"

"Does your, er, mistress often lock up people in rooms?"

She doesn't answer that, instead grabbing an unnaturally shaped kitchen instrument.

"Do not come any closer!"

Painfully, I sit up, rubbing my hip with a grimace, then raise both hands.

"No need to be scared. I'm not going to do anything. Also, you look pretty frightening with that thing," I say, pointing at the device.

And to my surprise, she looks genuinely pleased by that.

"I know. I practiced."

I consider asking why ever she would need to practice waving a giant spiky spoon around, but decide better.

"Is that infamous mistress around?"

"She and the young ladies went out on a call to the village."

"Right. Because that's an actual thing people do here..." I mutter to myself before speaking up. "And when will they be back?"

"Oh, not before some time, I believe."

"Right. Okay."

I rub a hand on my face.

"Is there anyone else I could speak to? A dad or something?"

The stricken look that appears on her face immediately makes me regret my question.

"I am afraid M. Allander passed away three years back. It has been a difficult time for the family..."

Damn. My hands still up, I move to sit on the bench by the table. She lowers her weapon when I sigh, too tired for whatever this is.

"Right. So no one is here. Except you," I add quickly, not wanting to slight her.

"Perhaps if you would wait a moment..."

"I'd rather go back, but sure, I'll wait," I snap half-heartedly.

That's enough to make her look scared once more. She raises her armed hand, which makes me slide back on the bench a little. A few moments of silence go by as I stare at the floor, feeling her eyes on me.

"So... You're Scottish?" I ask finally, more to make small talk than anything, because at this point, why not?

"Oh!" she says, surprised enough that she lowers her arm. "I am indeed! How did you know?"

"Your accent's a dead giveaway," I explain, rubbing my still throbbing temples, but she's already talking with enthusiasm, barely paying attention to my answer.

"I was born in Fife, in the village of Falkland!" she chatters as she sits next to me. "Oh, I miss it dearly! Have you ever travelled to Scotland, Miss...?"

"Max. And yes, quite a few times. I've been to Fife. It's lovely."

"It is truly the most beautiful place!"

Her excitement goes up the roof, and somehow, despite everything, I can't help but smile.

"My family lives in a small cottage by a farm, a most delightful place. And my brother and I used to go for long walks in the spring, gathering herbs and mushrooms! And in the winter, we played on the hills, rolling in the snow. How we laughed!"

Her expression darkens a little then, her voice wavering.

"Of course, it is beautiful here as well."

"Ha, sure. Sounds like you mean it," I say to tease her a little. "I didn't ask your name, by the way."

She seems to remember herself then because she jumps to her feet and bows. I immediately raise my hands in alarm.

"My name is Janet, Miss. Please call me Jeannie. The family does."

"But do you like Janet or Jeannie better?"

She hesitates an instant, wrenching her hands and not quite meeting my eyes.

"Janet, right?" I guess.

"It is my mother's name. I do cherish it dearly," she admits in a low voice.

"Okay, Janet you are then," I declare, standing up. "Now, Janet. As the mistress and the young ladies and whoever lives in this place won't be back for a while, would you mind if I grabbed something to eat?"

"Oh Miss, let me!"

She pushes on my shoulders, and I fall back on the bench with a startled laugh. Janet moves to the other side of the counter, barely sparing a glance at the spilled stew on the floor. But I'm a little bothered by the mess I made, so I get up to grab the already dirty rag hanging on the side of a basin.

"Miss, no, you cannot!" Janet exclaims as I lower myself on my knees, careful of my ankle.

"It's my fault you dropped some, so shush and let me scrub."

I'm almost surprised when she does shush and lets me scrub. I get to work with a light smile, finding myself relieved to be able to put a stop to my thoughts for a moment.

Soon after I'm done wiping up the damage, Janet sets down a steaming plate in front of me. I didn't realise how hungry I was until I lash out on it, inhaling the glorious stew in a matter of minutes.

"Okay, wow. That was incredible," I declare happily, scraping the bottom of the plate.

The blush on her cheeks tells me that compliments are the way to get more amazing food. I store that in a corner of my mind.

I just got up to put my plate aside when we hear a loud thud at the other side of the house, then a door slam. Janet straightens up immediately, throwing me a conflicted look.

Soon enough, I hear galloping in the corridor and find myself on the floor once more, crushed by a child-sized bundle.

Chapter Five

"Finally! You are awake!" Alice exclaims. "I wanted to see you before we had to leave, but Mamma said you were resting and that I should not bother you. But now you are awake! I have oh so many questions! Mamma said you—"

"Alice, would you please refrain from running away!"

The young woman from earlier enters the kitchen, her cheeks red and a frown on her face.

"You know it isn't polite to—"

She freezes when she sees me, clearly surprised.

"Hello there," I say, waving my spoon at her.

"What are you doing down here in your nightgown?" she exclaims. "I did not unlock the door for you to be walking around thoughtlessly. You should be resting!"

She moves closer, tilting my face up and pressing a soft hand on my forehead.

"You still have a fever and yet here you are, hardly dressed and with your feet bare!"

"Alma, look! I declare my feet free!" Alice announces from where she's now sitting on the floor, waving her second shoe.

"Jeannie, my mother did ask—" Alma says to Janet, who looks down instantly.

"Her name's Janet," I correct her before biting into the bun the maid set in front of me. "She likes it better."

The young woman drags her surprised look from me to Janet but is interrupted before she can say more.

"Jeannie, please hurry, we have a guest!"

Yet another woman enters the kitchen in a flurry of heavy skirts. Though she's a little smaller than Alma, the resemblance between the two of them—and Alice—is obvious. She stops dead when she sees me, and her astonished expression turns stony.

"How is she down here? And in her nightgown? Oh dear God, I do not have the time nor the wish to know what is happening here. M. Cuttingham is waiting in the parlour. Jeannie, would you be a dear and quickly bring us some tea?"

Interested—and relieved to be forgotten about for a little while—I settle on my bench and watch as madness unfolds. Janet flutters around the kitchen, adding baked biscuits to a tea tray while minding the surviving stew. The woman—whom I'm guessing to be the famous mistress and matriarch of the family—holds Alma close and whispers to her, her daughter nodding occasionally. I find Alice looking up at me from the floor, her expression curious.

"Why do you observe everything this way?" she asks.

"What way?"

"As if you were trying to understand something."

"There's quite a few things I'd like to understand, kiddo."

I watch the scene a little longer, impressed by Janet's dexterity and the way she moves around the other two, never in their way.

"Tea is ready, Ma'am," she announces, her cheeks red from the rush.

"Very well, thank you. Everyone hurry now! Alma, go sit with M. Cuttingham. Alice, would you get up from the floor, think of your dress! Jeannie, bring the tray in five minutes, but please keep the tea warm. And you..."

She squints at me. I try my best to answer with a convincing smile but end up mostly baring my teeth.

"Be kind enough as to stay here. I will handle this odd business later."

And with that, she gestures to Alice and follows Alma out of the kitchen, leaving me to wonder what just happened. Alice rolls her eyes exaggeratedly but complies after one last curious look at me. Poor Janet is holding the tea pot close to the fire to keep it warm, moving it away when the heat becomes unbearable.

"Why don't you just pour it back into the pan?" I ask, confused.

"Then it would steep too long."

"Does it actually matter? It's England. We're too polite not to drink the tea we're offered, even if it's disgusting."

Janet's giggles are replaced by a sharp hiss when her fingers slip from the rag she's using to hold the pot to the burning surface. She almost drops it, but I replace her hands with mine just in time and put down the pot on the table.

"Please hold it by the fire or it will get cold!" she begs.

"Dude, who cares? Come here."

I dip her hand into the bucket of cold water set by the counter, watching as relief fills her expression.

"I understand that it's your job and it's important, but think about yourself first, okay?"

Except she's not listening to me. Her eyes on the clock, she gasps, wrenching her hand from mine. But I catch it, submerging it back into the water.

"Nope, no way. Keep your hand in here or you'll get cloaks."

"But the mistress—"

"I'll bring the damn tea. Calm down."

"You cannot—"

"It's just a tray, it's not biochemistry."

"Bio—"

I seize my chance to grab the tray while she's distracted.

"Keep your hand in the water!" I instruct her before moving down the corridor, guiding myself with the voices I hear further in the house.

A few steps are enough to appreciate the difficulty of Janet's job, especially when combined with a twisted ankle. The tray is heavy and not quite stable, the floor uneven, the corridor dark. I take slow steps, spilling drops and losing a few biscuits on the way.

When I reach the door behind which voices can be heard, I let out a satisfied sigh. Which turns to an exasperated one when I realise that the door is closed, and both my hands are busy. I think about headbutting the door until someone opens it, but make the mature decision to simply put the tray down.

As soon as I push the door open, the conversation inside dies and all eyes fall on me. I crouch to pick up the tray, bothered by the hem of my silly dress.

"Er. Tea time?" I announce, stepping into the room.

Janet appears through an open door at the other end of the room, her face bright red and her hair dishevelled. I am glad to see that she wrapped her hand in a wet towel. Quickly reaching my side of the room, she takes the tray from my hands and sets it on the table between the two couches without a word.

I notice that everyone's eyes are still on me, accompanied by a variety of expressions. Hilarity for Alice, shock tinted with amusement for Alma, horror for the young man sitting next to her, and irritation for the mother.

It's when I meet her burning gaze that I realise I burst in uninvited.

"Ah, sorry, I should have knocked. I just wanted to help Janet out. The thing is, she bur—"

Janet doesn't let me finish, instead pushing me towards the door. Our rushed exit is followed by Alice's wild laughter.

***

Janet doesn't speak to me all the way back to the kitchen. I follow suit, both confused and a little vexed.

"I just wanted to help," I say to her turned back once I'm settled on the bench.

Janet drops the heavy ladle she's holding on the counter.

"You did not," she answers sharply. "The mistress will be angry that I let you show yourself like…"

I tilt my head, waiting for her to finish.

"Like what?" I ask when she doesn't.

"Like… Like a harlot!" she says in a breath, immediately covering her mouth with both hands, eyes wide.

"Ha."

I look down at my outfit, unsure why it deserves that much fuss.

"Because I'm in my pyjamas? That thing covers me down to my ankles. It's hardly indecent."

"Those are your night clothes. Which, as the name indicates, should be worn at night. Not to wander around the house when there are guests," an amused voice corrects me.

Alma comes to sit in front of me on the other side of the table, a light smile on her face.

"Mother is upset, and M. Cuttingham was unable to overcome your appearance. He left in a hurry. Alice, however, seems to find it quite amusing."

"And you?" I ask with a grin.

"A show of indecency in the family parlour surely does not help my prospects," she says with a severe expression I don't buy. "However, all is well now. We explained to M. Cuttingham that you suffered a fall on your head and that you haven't been quite right since. Proper manners seem to evade you."

"I'll let you know I'm super proper. The properest. Most proper. Whatever," I conclude with a dismissive wave. "I walked around in a really thick and covering nightgown. I didn't do a striptease on the piano."

Alma stares at me as she seems to debate whether to ask what the hell I'm talking about, but apparently decides against it.

"Anyhow, you cannot possibly stay like this. You need clothes. *Proper* clothes," she says with a smile before turning to Janet. "Jea—Janet. Would you be kind enough to find our guest a fitting outfit in my wardrobe?"

"Of course, Miss," Janet answers with a small bow before gesturing at me to follow.

"Oh, and please also find appropriate undergarments. We do not want M. Cuttingham to choke on his biscuit again," Alma adds, barely concealing her smile.

I get up with a sigh.

"Fine. But I'm keeping my own knickers."

Chapter Six

"Nope. No way. That's not happening."

"Miss, you must!"

Janet holds the corset up, straps undone, the front open.

"There's no way I'm wearing this torture device. Do you want me to be unable to breathe, is that it?"

"It would solve our predicament," she mumbles darkly.

"Hey! Rude."

I cross my arms, resolute.

"I refuse. Corsets are an oppression tool against women."

Janet just stares at me blankly.

"I don't even need it. Look at me!"

I spin on myself, highlighting my lanky frame and lack of curves. Janet studies me carefully.

"I suppose you could do without... For now. Mrs Allander will have to decide."

I smirk smugly as she puts the corset away. Unfortunately, I'm unable to escape the long-sleeved dress she chooses after one disbelieving look at my tattoos, and the thick chemise under. That's too many layers for one outfit. Janet slips flat shoes at my feet, and I could be wearing none, it wouldn't feel much different. She tries to tame my short, uneven hair with a few ribbons, but quickly gives up to my greatest relief.

Once she deems she tormented me enough, Janet leads me back to the parlour where the family is gathered. The mother seems to have been expecting me because she barely waits until I'm seated next to Alice to begin her questioning.

"Would you kindly tell me your name?"

"Max. Max Jones."

"Max... I see. Well. My name is Mrs Adriana Allander. Those are two of my three daughters. Alma, my second, and Alice, my youngest. My eldest daughter, Ann, is currently travelling with a neighbour and will not return for another two months."

She pauses there, making it clear that she doesn't expect me to still be here to meet her eldest progeny. That makes two of us.

To relieve the tension, I consider commenting on the love of the letter A in the family, but decide it probably wouldn't do much good. So I nod silently, inviting her to continue.

"Alma tells me Alice found you in the field yesterday in the late afternoon. You seemed lost, were dressed in the most peculiar manner and had hurt your ankle. I do hope you feel better."

"I—"

"However," she interrupts.

Ok then.

"You must understand that it is unusual for us to welcome a stranger under our roof. Especially one that seems to have emerged from someplace unknown... I do consider my daughters' safety above all."

She holds my gaze, her expression turning more intrigued than wary.

"Yet... Although you seem to have acquired strange manners, my daughters trust you mean no harm. That you are simply lost. What sort of mother would I be if I didn't have faith in my daughters' instinct? A question remains, however... Will you be worth of this trust?"

I glance at Alice, who moved a little closer and pushed my sleeve up to follow the lines of my tattoos with the tips of her fingers. Alma gazes at us with a calm expression, the same light smile as earlier playing on her lips.

"I am lost," I admit, frowning. "And I don't know how to go back yet. But I want to, and soon. And of course, I don't mean any harm. Your daughters were kind enough to help me. Not everyone would have done the same."

Mrs Allander sighs and pats Alma's hand.

"I must say, you are not the first stray my girls brought home."

Taking my indignation as confusion, Alma points at a large black mass looming under the piano.

"Please meet Fitz," she says. "Our cat."

"M. Cuttingham tried to pat him, but Fitz dislikes it, so he spat on him," Alice informs me, laughter in her voice. "Now, Fitz will be mad for at least three hours, till we serve him dinner."

"Right, cool... So..." I say hesitantly, to steer the conversation back to my situation. "Does it mean I can stay here for a bit while I sort things out? Do I have to sleep under the piano with the rest of the strays?"

The shadow of a smile appears on Mrs Allander's face, but she forces a sober expression.

"You may stay for a little while, yes, to... sort things out, as you put it. At least till your ankle is better. And you are welcome to remain in

Ann's room. I did have a few of her belongings removed, but of course, should you need anything, do not hesitate to ask."

"That's, er, very kind," I say, getting up to curtsy clumsily as I saw Janet do, for good measure. "Thank you."

Mrs Allander studies my mediocre attempt before turning to Alma.

"Dearest, please find our guest a corset for tomorrow. I already fear her nightgown will be at the centre of conversations for days."

Not giving me time to protest, Mrs Allander grabs a little bell on the side table and rings it. A few seconds later, Janet enters the room, wiping her hands on her apron.

"Ma'am?"

"Jean—"

"I do believe our Jeannie would prefer to be called Janet from now on, Mother," Alma says.

Janet glances my way briefly with a small smile that Mrs Allander catches, looking between the two of us.

"I see. Well, Janet, would you please set a plate at the dinner table for our guest?"

"Right away, Ma'am."

Janet exits the room, leaving us to sit in an awkward silence. I look around the parlour, trying to find something to say.

"So..." I start, unsure what's about to come out of my mouth, but Mrs Allander unknowingly saves the day.

"If you would like to rest before dinner, you are most welcome to retire to your room. Alice shall fetch you when it is time."

I'm already up on my feet and halfway out of the room by the time she finishes her sentence.

"Cool, awesome. See you later," I rush to say as I disappear from their sight.

Stumbling in the corridor, I try to find my way back to the staircase, my eyes not used to the darkness. Instinctively, I pat the wall for the light switch and immediately snort, then sigh. This is all ridiculous.

Taking a turn right, I soon reach the staircase illuminated by a single window, like a beacon in times of need. I climb carefully, my unarmed feet forward, cursing under my breath the whole time.

When I step on the landing, I finally take a moment to pay attention to what I ignored during my first trips down. The corridor stretches south, the eldest daughter's room at the end of it and several more wooden doors punctuating the lightly coloured walls.

Slowly, I walk the length of it, briefly stopping at the few painted portraits hanging between the windows, most of them of Mrs Allander with a tall man with dark hair and a funky moustache. Probably the deceased M. Allander Janet mentioned earlier.

I keep moving, only pausing to peak through the gap of an opened door at what I assume to be Alice's room. The mess in it surely feels like the mayhem only a child could create. The two following doors are closed and even though I'm wildly curious, I'm not too keen on invading their privacy.

So I retreat to the absent daughter's room, whose name I already forgot. Definitively something starting with *A*, though. I walk to the desk, poking half-heartedly at the papers on it now that I know that Mrs Allander did clean away anything of importance.

Next, I try the window to maybe spot anything of use outside, but there's nothing except a neglected garden and the surrounding woods. It's a little too quiet, as if the house was cut away from the world.

As I look away to wallow in my defeat, my frown vanishes when I find my own clothes still where they were earlier, cleanly folded, shirt on top, jeans last. Forgetting where I am for a moment, I consider putting them on and returning downstairs to join the family. Maybe they would think I lost my mind. Or maybe they'd believe me if I told them everything.

Weighing my options, I hesitate. Is it a risk worth taking? Shouldn't I instead focus on the woman or the painting? Except I have zero idea who and what they really are and even less where to find them. At least, the family is here, right now. Maybe they know something...

I spend a while trying to come up with explanations for my little problem that sound sane enough to be plausible. And each time, I reach the same conclusion.

I can't say any of that.

If I knew anything real about this era, maybe I could figure out what to do. But I don't and it's clear I'm in way over my head.

But.

If I were to make up a story as to how I came here—omitting the time travel side of it, obviously— and stick to it while staying on the Allanders' good side, the solution is bound to show up, right?

Before my inside voice has time to make up its mind, there's a loud knock on my door and Alice's voice telling me to come down for dinner.

So I take a deep breath in. And I jump into the unknown.

Chapter Seven

Alice is waiting by the door when I come out, humming softly to herself. She stops when our eyes meet.

"Do you often have dinner where you are from?" she asks casually, as if the question made sense.

"You mean, like... Do we eat?" is my perplexed answer. "It's kind of essential to survive, so... yes?"

She leads the way down the stairs, fingers tapping on the guardrail.

"And what do you eat?"

"Er. Probably the same as you?"

I'm not quite sure where this is going, but we're reaching the end of the staircase and I'm hoping the dinner table isn't too far away.

"Have you ever eaten insects? Or animals you hunted yourself?"

"You do realise I grew up in London, right?"

"But your arms—"

"Yes, well, that's something different."

She pauses then and I'm hoping it means the conversation is over, but it seems she was only thinking.

"But do you know how to hunt? And fish? And find your way in the dark with only the stars to guide you?"

"Look, Alice. I'm not Davy Crockett or a girl scout or whatever."

Stopping, she tilts her head to study me for a moment.

"Perhaps mamma is right. You *have* lost your mind."

Then she simply resumes walking and humming, leaving me behind, stunned. I almost follow my impulse to return to the bedroom because if a kid can unsettle me that much, I'm clearly unprepared for the adults.

But Alice calls my name from somewhere on the right, and I let out a deep sigh before raising my chin and following.

I enter a room I haven't been to yet. It's centred by a heavy table covered with a white embroidered tablecloth, plates and dishes, and there's only one free chair left in front of Alma and between Alice and Mrs Allander, who's presiding. Because that doesn't feel intimidating at all. Regardless, I sit, avoiding everyone's eyes for as long as possible.

"I trust you managed to rest a little?" Mrs Allander asks politely.

I nod without a word, pretending to find the setting of the table fascinating. And honestly... It is a little. It seems like a lot of food for only five people, and everything looks delicious. When I make a note to thank Janet, I realise something.

"Janet isn't eating with us?"

Mrs Allander studies me carefully before answering.

"It is not in our customs, no."

"But she cooked all of this, though, right? She should get to enjoy it?"

"It would not be appropriate for her to dine with us."

"But—" I start to protest.

Alma cuts in, her tone kind.

"It seems the customs you are used to are different from ours. Pray tell, where do you come from?"

"I, hm... Well, actually, I..."

I look away for a second, regretting wasting my time with useless thoughts earlier instead of actually planning a decent story. My eyes fall on a pile of books set on a low table by the chimney and I smile victoriously as a plan forms in my head. That's it. I'll just improvise from books. I knew reading so much would come in handy, eventually. So I clear my throat and let my imagination run free.

"I'm British, but my parents passed away abroad when I was young, and I was sent to an orphanage. A good friend of my dad's found me when I was around 10 and told me he was leaving England. He asked me to join him, and we went to... To Canada! To a small island on the east of the continent, where we settled on a lovely little farm with green gables and a lake of shining water and stuff."

I look around at the Allanders' expressions to figure out whether they believe me so far. Alice is hanging on to my every word, but Alma and Mrs Allander show nothing but polite interest. When I run a hand through my hair to take a moment to think, lines of my tattoos appear in sight, reminding me to include them.

"As I grew up, I started to help my sort-of dad around the farm, and we sometimes had to do business with sea merchants. Not pirates!" I add quickly when I see Alice's face brightening with excitement. "Because they brought back plants we could grow from their trips. And eventually, I became friends with them and got those ta—those marks on my arms. Like they have."

I lean back on my chair with the satisfaction of a lie well weaved. Alice lets me bask in the illusion for a minute before chiming in.

"Did you not say earlier that you grew up in London?"

My smile falls.

"Ah. Yes. And by that, I meant... The orphanage was in London. So I did grow up there a little! After that, I lived in many places. So many. So you know."

I wave my hand as if to dismiss her question.

"What a fascinating childhood you seem to have had," Mrs Allander remarks. "Yet it does not explain how you come to be here today."

"Indeed, it does not. Well, the reason behind that is quite simple. I... I was looking for... my mother."

"The mother who passed away?" Alma asks, and I could swear she looks a little amused.

"Yes, that one. Turns out she's alive somewhere in London, which is what my second dad told me briefly before he himself... passed away."

I pause and look down sadly, as if grieving for a beloved father figure that was taken too soon. Alice squeezes my hand.

"Thank you, thank you. And so, alone in the world and longing for my mother, I left Canada to search for her. But when I got here, I was attacked by... By miscreants!" I say, forcing a distraught expression.

"Is that right?" Mrs Allander comments. "And those men are the reason why you were alone in the field, dressed in mannish clothes, with no idea where you were?"

"Exactly. But luckily for me, your daughters found me and now, I'm here."

I nod satisfyingly when Alice looks at me in awe.

"Quite the adventure," Mrs Allander says mildly. "But it seems to solve our predicament."

I frown, confused.

"Sorry?"

"Well, we simply have to help you find the mother for whom you feel such longing. Then you can be on your way."

"Oh, but mamma, couldn't we keep her?" Alice complains.

"Dearest, she isn't a toy for you to keep," Alma says, definitively amused now.

I'm struggling to make up an answer that would get them off my scent.

"Ah yes, but you see... I don't know her name."

Mrs Allander stares at me, lips curving subtly.

"Well, isn't that unfortunate?"

She exchanges a long look with Alma, who eventually nods. Mrs Allander lets out a thoughtful hum.

"Considering your... tragic circumstances, we couldn't possibly leave you to fend for yourself in a world where miscreants attack young ladies. So our previous agreement stands. You are welcome to remain with us till a solution can be found."

The slight guilt I felt at lying so blatantly vanishes, her words making it more than clear that she does not buy my story. Yet, they're letting me stay so I don't push my luck any further, simply nodding and whispering a thank you.

"Very well. Now that this is settled, shall we dine?" Mrs Allander says.

Alma takes one of the dishes and passes it to her mother, who pours her a glass of wine in exchange. I feel a tug on my sleeve and detach my eyes from them to turn to Alice.

"Did you learn how to ride a horse on your farm?" she asks, genuine curiosity brightening her voice.

I glance at Mrs Allander, who nods subtly at me, as if to allow me and my stories.

"Well no, not on the farm," I start, "but I did ride horses once, when..."

The dinner goes on like this, with more stories, mostly real. I try my best to stick closer to the truth without revealing anything damming and it turns out to be an absolute mind-twister. Once all the 21st century elements removed, my stories sound pretty bland to my ears. But it doesn't seem to bother Alice, however, who asks endless questions until Mrs Allander forces her to go to bed.

I yawn widely myself then, more tired than I realised, and wonder how to leave for my room without seeming rude. Mrs Allander must have noticed, however, because she throws me a considerate look.

"We shall see you in the morning, Max. There are matters to be settled."

I nod thankfully and make my way upstairs, feet light as I pass Alice's room. The door closed behind me, I lean against it and take a deep breath in. A warm feeling curls in me as I remember Alice's laugh at my stories, Alma's measured curiosity, Mrs Allander's final smile at me...

The warmth is still here when I change into my horrible nightgown and settle under the bed cover, wondering what all of this means.

Chapter Eight

I wake up abruptly, confused by the absence of noise. I can't hear my flatmate moving around the kitchen, slamming the fridge door more violently that needed, nor the hiss of the kettle. Instead of children screaming in the street on their way to school, I hear the soft chirping of birds and a breeze coming through the gap of an open window...

As my vision settles, it takes a second longer for my brain to catch up, events from the previous days coming back to me.

Ah. Yes.

I search for anything that could indicate the time before getting out of bed unwillingly to look outside. The sun is barely up, soft mist covering the edge of the forest. There's nothing ruining the peace of the moment, no car, no plane roaring in the sky, no music playing from a phone or passers-by with aggressively loud voices. It's beautiful and quiet. Soothing, even.

Following an impulse, I slip my shirt over my nightdress and grab my boots before leaving the room and going downstairs as quietly as possible. I turn the key in the lock of the front door and twist the handle, taking a deep breath in as fresh morning air hits my nose.

Once outside, I put on my boots, carefully tying the laces around my bad ankle, before studying my surroundings and wondering where to go first. I notice a vaguely familiar small path weaving through the trees and wonder if it's the one leading back to the field.

Only one way to find out.

But just before entering the forest, I turn around, taking in the house for the first time. Based on the inside, I knew it wasn't a huge house, but it's still quite sizeable for a single family compared to the standards of my day. But mostly, it's just... Well, it's perfectly lovely.

There's ivy climbing on each side of the door up to the first floor, where a few windows are—the ones from the corridor most probably, as my room has a view of the garden. Brownish red tiles, the walls a faded colour between pink and orange, the white painted frames of the windows and the dark wooden door...

It looks cosy and inviting, just what a home should be.

Almost reluctantly, I detach my eyes from it and make my way through the forest. Emerging on the other side confirms my assumption. It is the field. I take a few wobbly steps, not that surprised anymore that I managed to twist my ankle when I first landed here. I look up at the sky then, wondering stupidly if I fell down from it or simply blinked into existence. But it doesn't really matter because whatever the answer is, it wouldn't change a thing.

I move forward slowly, eyes on the ground, to maybe spot something that could belong to me and have fallen when I did. I'm not sure how much time passes as I comb the field, my limp worsening with each minute. The sun is fully up by the time I accept it's meaningless. There's nothing here, no hint, no explanation, no guidance.

It would be easy to surrender to my panic at being stuck here, helpless, and moan about the weird turn my life took. But instead, I remember my certainty that a solution is bound to come up, eventually. All I have to do is wait patiently and keep up appearances for as long as it takes. That should be fun.

Chapter Nine

In an unspoken agreement, Mrs Allander grants me two whole weeks to find my footing and I spend most of that time with Alice, who's only too happy to have found a willing playmate. Her ability to come up with all sorts of stories based on books she read or anecdotes she heard fascinates me. I should have asked her to make up a background for my own past. It would have been much more believable.

Thanks to our games, I learn my way around the house and the garden, a little sad to see up close the latter's state of neglect. More than once, I wonder how much work it would take to restore it, before reminding myself that I'm not here to stay.

The first few days, Alma keeps an eye on me when I'm outside with Alice, possibly still a little wary. I can't blame her for that, but I still feel relieved when I notice one morning that she hasn't followed us. We haven't talked much in private since that very first day, mostly because the chores Mrs Allander gives me usually dispatch me to the kitchen with Janet.

Rapidly, I notice that those chores seem to always coincide with visits from neighbours and well, I can't say I mind. Lodging with a family in the 19th century is one thing; having to actually join the society of the time is a whole different matter.

The Allanders begin to accept my oddities faster than expected, even asking questions when they don't understand a word or a turn of phrase. Surprisingly, it's Janet who gets accustomed the quickest, possibly because of all those hours spent together in the kitchen. It was unavoidable that we speak. That's also when I learn that there's more to her than the shy and obedient appearance she assumes while in the presence of the family.

From her teasing and biting remarks—that I had already experienced during the Great Corset Debate—it seems she feels more at ease with me than with the Allanders. Probably because she knows I can't fire her. I like being the only one witnessing this different part of her. And I like that she feels comfortable enough with me to act naturally. It makes those common chores much more fun.

As for Mrs Allander... While a little hesitant at first, she seems to eventually tolerate my presence amongst them. After a week or so, she even begins to leave me alone in the house sometimes—in the care of Janet—for me to "make progress on my situation".

And I try. I really do.

I make dozens of lists, trying to find reasons, ideas for my return. I walk back to the field again and again, jumping up and down and leaving no stone unturned, sometimes observed by a very puzzled Janet. I try magic words, demands, even desperate clumsy prayers. Obviously, none of that works, the last one least of all.

So as the two weeks come to a close, I'm nowhere near finding a way back. And from the slivers of conversation I catch between Alma and Mrs Allander one afternoon, it seems my reprieve is also ending.

Which Mrs Allander confirms one morning at the very end of the second week.

"Our neighbours have been wondering about you," she explains. "It seems tales of your nightgown have circulated, and it is crucial that they do not stand."

I wince at that.

"I don't think meeting anyone would be a good idea," I say truthfully. "I wouldn't know how to act or what to say. It would just be a succession of humiliating mistakes."

"That is why Alma is to teach you the proper manner to behave in polite society from tomorrow."

I throw a look of betrayal at Alma, who has the nerve to smile teasingly. Redirecting my attention to Mrs Allander's determined expression, I sigh.

"I don't have a choice, do I?"

"I do hope you will comply of your own good will," Mrs Allander says with a sharp smile that makes it clear that indeed, I do not have a choice.

***

"Now, for today's lesson. As you enter the room, nod politely, a smile perhaps if it seems appropriate. Then, you must wait until you are invited to sit," Alma explains.

She takes a few light steps into the room, her eyes demurely lowered the whole time, before curtsying. When Mrs Allander gestures towards the couch, Alma takes a seat, her knees gathered on one side, then rests her hands palms down on her perfectly folded skirt.

This is ridiculous.

I grunt and move forward, my steps heavy and restricted due to the flat shoes I'm still not used to. Mrs Allander's disapproval exudes from her like acid, but Alma looks at me with an encouraging smile. She rests a hand on my arm when I finally drop down next to her, as elegantly as I am able to. Which is not at all.

"Well. Practice makes perfect, let us hope," Mrs Allander says after a sigh.

"I'm entering a room. I don't understand why I need to pretend like I'm walking on thin air," I grumble.

"A discreet yet elegant entrance is the mark of a lady."

"I'm hardly a lady."

"Which is what we have been trying to correct."

"I never said I wanted to be one," I note irritably. "I'd rather find my way back."

Mrs Allander's severe expression softens a little at that.

"I know, dear. But you said yourself you do not know how to. So, for now, we have more pressing matters to focus on."

"We cannot afford to keep you hidden much longer now that your ankle is better. You must appear in society soon, to prove you aren't as uncivilised as they seem to believe," Alma says with the teasing smile that's often turned my way.

For once, I don't find it charming.

"Uncivilised?" I repeat, offended.

"Well, the Misses Harrington may have seen you covered in dirt when you fell, that day we started on the garden. Rumours may have spread…"

"They seriously have nothing better to do?"

"Regardless," Mrs Allander interrupts, "we have all been invited to tea by Lady Cuttingham at the end of the coming week."

She exchanges a serious look with Alma, who lowers her eyes, her smile vanishing.

"It is imperative that you are ready, Max. We must make a good impression."

"I mean, I could come and be silent?" I say, trying to be helpful. "If I master how to sit properly, all I have to do is stare at the floor and giggle or nod when required, right?"

Mrs Allander seems amused at that.

"I have not known you long, yet I struggle to believe you could keep silent for the entirety of a visit."

"Well, depends. Are we talking about a quick 'hey, how are you' visit? Or an extensively boring conversation about weather, pigs and whatnots?"

"Pigs and whatnots!" Alice confirms gleefully.

I wince.

"I guess I could... try. To be nice and all."

"And to be...?" Mrs Allander insists.

"To be... ladylike," I answer through gritted teeth, almost choking on the word.

Then, deciding I had enough for the day, I jump to my feet.

"Right, this is all obscene. Alice, come! Let's cause some mayhem outside."

"Yee haw!" she says, already running towards the corridor.

"I may have taught her that," I explain innocently to her surprised mother and amused sister. "I promise to be on my best behaviour from tomorrow, but for now, I need to cleanse myself from all that. Maybe even scare a Miss Harrington or two if I'm lucky..."

***

As promised, from the next day and for the rest of that week, I learn to bow and laugh prettily when required. I learn how to eat cake like a well-behaved human being and to hold my teacup as it were breakable.

Which it is, as I discover when Fitz the Cat decides to impose his not so insignificant weight on my lap just when I take a sip.

We spend almost every afternoon trying to turn me into something I'm not, and somehow... I'm having fun? To me, those rules are out-dated and senseless, yes, but it's increasingly fascinating to see how the women of the house have bent them to take control of their lives, despite customs and expectations.

From comments I overheard after one of their visits to the village on market day, houses with only women seem to often be frowned upon. But I can't imagine this one in any other way.

Mrs Allander is the parent, the master and mistress of the house. The other three are her closest advisors in everything. Each one of them participates actively, from household chores to more important issues. Mrs Allander hides nothing from her daughters—even from Janet, for most things. She trusts them openly and entirely. Her gentle dedication to her family reveals itself as the days go by, and I can't help but be impressed by her.

Quickly enough, I let myself be dragged into their routine, finding my place in its well-oiled clogs. As the week closes, I realise I haven't thought once about how to go back, too distracted by chores, chats and garden work with Alma, games with Alice—and sometimes Fitz when he's in the mood—lady lessons, family dinners...

For the first time in a long time, I fall asleep easily each night.

Chapter Ten

I'm more than nervous on the day of our visit, because so much could go wrong so easily. When we reach the Cuttingham's house, I wipe my sweaty hands on my skirts before we enter the parlour as poised and elegant as can be, Mrs Allander in the lead, followed by the rest of us. Alice won't let go of my clammy hand, though I'm not sure which one of us needs it more. We curtsy, and smile, and exchange "how do you do's". I sit well enough, only fussing a little with my skirt to make it look like Alma's, which, yet again, falls down perfectly.

Mrs Allander introduces me as a distant relation from Canada on a visit to England. I do my best to smile convincingly, remembering not to show my teeth as Alma taught me.

To my relief, I quickly find that I'm not expected to participate in the conversation, relinquished by the hostess to the role of flowerpot. When I feel Alice moving restlessly by my side, I tickle her ribs, but stop when she lets out a wild giggle that causes Mrs Allander to shoot daggers at us.

I barely pay attention to the conversation, more interested by the heavy and tasteless decoration because who knew one could own so many stuffed parrots? I make a note to myself to look up if they were a mark of wealth after I get back to the 21st century and the debatable wonders of the Internet.

The right wall is covered with portraits of family members displaying condescending expressions, just like the one our current hostess is wearing. She sits straight in her chair, her eyes cold and her mouth in a fine line as she pretends to listen to Mrs Allander. I recognise the young man standing up between the two couches as the shy one I scared with my frilly nightgown. When I grin at him, he turns red and looks anywhere but at me.

But just when I start to congratulate myself on behaving, things deteriorate. We're invited to stay over for dinner, an unexpected honour apparently. Except we haven't covered dinner etiquette in our lessons yet. As we sit down around the table, I throw panicked looks at Alma, who answers with a calm and reassuring smile. It's not enough compared to all the spoons and forks laid in front of me, though. Also plates, plural?

The confusion lasts past the entrée—I roll my eyes at the posh tone of the hostess when she announces it—until I start to relax and simply copy everything the Allanders do. Still, Alma covers a laugh with her hand when Alice has to correct me quite firmly on which spoon to use for the soup thing we're served between courses.

That's when I become able to focus on the conversation. And immediately regret it.

"After the wedding, I expect the happy couple to live for at least a year in our family home, in Newcastle. It is the most exquisite house for newlyweds. I, of course, will accompany them, as our bride will require guidance to settle in her new life."

I look between the old woman whose name I can't quite remember and Mrs Allander's blank expression.

"Well, of course," the latter says in a syrupy tone I'm surprised to hear from her. "You certainly are an endless source of good taste and thoughtful advice."

I choke on my peas and immediately hide my hilarity by drinking a large gulp of water.

"Sorry," I say in an apologetic tone when I find all eyes on me. "That was a slippery one!"

Alma seems glad of the distraction I caused. The old woman at the head of the table, however, not so much. She squints at me.

"And pray tell, young lady, what are your thoughts on what a first home should be for newlyweds?"

I give it a second of thought, aware of Mrs Allander's heavy stare on me.

"Ah, well. I guess it should be someplace where they both feel comfortable? Also, a place that belongs entirely to them, where they can start their own story?"

I distinctively hear a sigh of relief coming from my two eldest housemates when the woman nods sagely at my improvised answer.

"Of course, of course. And the wife must be careful to keep their nest warm and welcoming, so that the husband will want to spend time inside."

At that, I can't hold back a wince, and my self-control crumbles.

"How can they both be feeling comfortable if one has to work harder to turn their home into some sort of trap to keep the other in?" I wonder aloud. "Creating the perfect space is a shared chore that belongs equally to both spouses."

Mrs Allander's hard stare is back. I answer it with an innocent shrug and attack another spoonful of peas.

"With such a mind, you are not bound to find a decent husband anytime soon, dear one," the old hag says sharply.

"Oh no, woe is me," I mutter under my breath.

Alice giggles, dragging the woman's attention to her. I feel her freeze on her chair.

"What about you, young Alice? Are you eager about your own future prospects?"

Astonished and disgusted, I drop my spoon on the table, peas rolling everywhere.

"She's 12!"

"Max," Mrs Allander says, a soft warning. "I believe it was innocently meant. After all, this talk of weddings must awaken questions in Alice's mind as well."

Alice is looking down at the table, on the verge of tears. In front of me, Alma is resolutely staring at her own collection of cutlery.

"Wait, sorry, what?" I say, realising something. "I think I missed a bit there. Who's getting married?"

"Why, young Alma and my dear nephew of course!" the old woman replies, her tone too victorious for my taste.

"Alma and your... nephew..."

I stare at the only man present, who yet again looks red and terrified to be at the centre of attention. I think back on his presence at the house on my first full day. The multiple "important visits" Alma and Mrs Allander made leading to this week. I remember hushed conversations between the two. What I can't remember is Alma ever talking about him or expressing any sort of interest.

"That's a joke, right?" I let out, shocked at the thought that Alma, bright and wonderful Alma, is expected to marry this boring, invisible man.

"It most certainly is not!" the old woman says, outraged.

She grabs a bell on the table and rings it more times than needed.

"Henry, please show our guests to the door," she orders when the servant man comes into the room. "It seems our foreign friend is quite tired and has forgotten her place."

Angry, I don't make her ask twice and storm out of the room before poor Henry can even open the door.

***

"But it makes no sense!" I protest, bursting into the kitchen.

Janet lunges to her feet, a worried look on her face at my raised voice.

"I disagree," Mrs Allander says calmly.

Alma and Alice follow us in, the oldest taking off her gloves and hat, the youngest dropping in front of the fire to disrupt Fitz's nap.

"I don't understand how you can ask that from Alma! She's great and smart, and that guy is just... sort of alive. He doesn't deserve her!"

"My mother did not ask," Alma corrects me. "It was my idea."

"But..."

She holds my stare, chin raised, daring me to continue.

I learned just enough from books and films to know what is expected from women in this era and I used to assume it was also what they wanted. But as I got to know Alma those past weeks, it became clear how wrong I was.

When in public, Alma is seen as the perfect figure of feminine grace and politeness. But in private, she enjoys getting her hands dirty in the garden, she sasses me with an ease yet to be matched, she loves to play with her kid sister. She is profoundly devoted to her family and...

"You're doing this for your family," I say, realization dawning.

I take her lack of answer for a yes and look between her and Mrs Allander.

"But... But why? Is it a money thing? A reputation thing?"

Seeing the look they exchange, I seem to have struck close to the truth, yet they don't answer. Mrs Allander throws a quick look at Alice, who's contentedly playing with the cat, and clears her throat.

"It hardly matters. I doubt Lady Cuttingham will soon ask us all to tea again," she says, looking straight at me. "We have you to thank for this."

I feel a sharp stab of guilt when she leaves the room without another word, Alma following her in silence.

***

The guilt hasn't vanished hours later as I'm lying in bed, restless.

Exasperated, I get up to go steal wine or food from the kitchen, whatever is closest. But as I pass Alma's room, I notice the flick of a light through the gap under the door.

Taking a long breath in, I knock gently. There's the soft flutter of feet on the floor and I step back when the door opens just an inch, revealing Alma's face. Her frown worsens when she recognises me.

"It is quite late, Max..."

"I know, I know, sorry," I whisper back. "I was on my way to the kitchen, but then I saw you were awake, and I just... Can we talk?"

For a second, she seems on the verge of saying no, but then opens the door wider. As I come in, she hurries back to her bed, covering herself up to her neck with the sheets.

"You're cold?" I ask, surprised.

"I tend to be easily cold, yes. Sue me," she says with a slight smile, making me grin by stealing one of my favourite expressions.

"Between Alice and you, seems like I have a bad influence..." I joke back, eager to resume our normal relationship.

She doesn't react to my attempt, however, instead looking down at the frayed threads on her bedsheets.

"Right," I sigh. "Listen, earlier…"

"It pained me to hear you judging us. Judging me," she interrupts, still not meeting my gaze.

"I didn't mean to—"

"I may not know where you really come from, but I do know that you find our way of living strange and unworthy of you."

"That's not—"

"It is," she states sharply. "But you must understand it is *our* way. And there is no changing that, whether we wish it or not."

The bitterness is clear in her voice. I feel sorry and angry and frustrated all at once to see someone so wonderful having to settle for so little. Someone I came to care a lot about, I realise.

Despite the chill between us, when I sit by her side against the headboard, she lays her head on my shoulder.

"I ruined your chances with M. Boring-ham, didn't I…"

Her chuckle dissolves in a sigh.

"I do believe it can be repaired. It is Lady Cuttingham who needs to be soothed, and I am not afraid of a challenge."

"That old crone…" I mutter sombrely, faking a shiver. "When did sir Shy propose to you by the way?"

"He did not propose yet. But he will, of that I am sure."

"Oh? But the way his aunt spoke about it, I thought…"

"She certainly wishes it."

A moment of silence passes between us.

"And there really isn't any… prospect you would actually like? Or at least, like more?"

"There hasn't been these past three years. None with the title and fortune of M. Cuttingham."

"Why is it always the worst men that are the richest..." I mutter.

"To torture us women, quite obviously," Alma deadpans, a light smile playing on her lips.

Surprised, I snort, but sober up when something she said strikes me.

"Three years... Is that when—"

"Our father died, yes."

"Oh." Then. "It's all related, isn't it? Your father, the need to marry for money?"

Alma's considering look confirms my guess.

"Well, yes, it is. Our situation is... peculiar," she says slowly.

"What do you mean?"

"If things were to change unexpectedly, we would be left with nothing if we do not marry."

"I'm not sure I understand."

"This house, where we grew up and always lived, does not belong to us. We remain here at the courtesy of the distant cousin to whom it was entailed after our father's passing. As he did not need it for himself, he granted us his permission to stay."

"But that's good, isn't it? Why the need to marry then?"

"Our cousin allowed us to stay on the condition that when my sisters and I are married, my mother will leave to reside with one of us. The house will return to him then."

"But... But that's unfair!" I sputter indignantly. "That's not his family home and I'm guessing he got it just because he's a man? Why would he want to take it if he doesn't need it?"

"Because he can," Alma sighs. "Our hope now is that one of our husbands will be generous enough to purchase the house deed from him, so that it can stay in our family. I know it would break my father's heart to see it taken from us."

"But he didn't take any measure to prevent that from happening?"

A small, affectionate smile appears on Alma's lips at my question.

"Although he was a most loving and caring father, I cannot say he had a strong inclination to think of the future."

"When it could have helped avoid that sort of situation, it would have been useful though..." I hear myself mumble before throwing an apologetic look to Alma. "Sorry. That was rude."

"What is done is done. Now, we must focus on the future."

We stay silent for a moment, both busy with our own thoughts.

"When my father left us..." Alma starts, "we stopped truly living for some time. It felt as if everything between us, everything that made us a family, had vanished. To this day, I do not know that we truly returned to how we were before. We stopped receiving guests for a long time, we kept to ourselves. When Janet came to us, a year after his passing perhaps, she found the house in such a disarray that I believed she wouldn't stay. But she did. And Alice helped us accept our reality. She was young then, but resilient. One day, she made it clear that we must go on, so we did. It was harder for my mother, but I believe that slowly, she is getting better despite all the worries we now have to face. I think she has found a purpose."

I keep silent for a moment, looking for the right words, but I feel deeply unqualified for that kind of talk.

"I know saying it doesn't change a thing, but I... I'm sorry all that happened to you."

"Thank you, Max," Alma answers gently. "But know you are also helping, in your own way."

Now, that genuinely confuses me.

"I was under the impression I was doing the exact opposite?"

"Today set aside, having you here brings life back into our home. And when you asked to restore the garden... It was my father's garden, you see, and I remember it plentiful and so full of colours. I cannot wait for the day when it is so again."

"Oh."

It shouldn't touch me so much to hear that I'm helping, even in a small way, that I'm doing something good. And yet.

"I'll do my best," I mumble embarrassingly, trying to shove back my feelings into the dark void from where they escaped.

Alma simply smiles at me, and hours go by as we stay up, talking quietly until the candle flickers out.

Chapter Eleven

When I wake up in my own bed the following morning, I feel already exhausted by the amount of apologising I have to do, starting with Mrs Allander. But as I enter the kitchen, she welcomes me with a kind smile and asks me to help carry a tray without even a slight mention of the previous day.

Only too happy not to face her disappointment again, I follow her with a bounce in my step, carefully avoiding the more uneven tiles in the corridor.

We sit around the table, Alice already trying to pick food on my plate and starting a fork fight that I let her win, as I do every morning. Alma smiles at our antics but turns to her mother when the latter clears her throat and puts down her fork.

I immediately close my eyes and wince, but turn towards her to receive my sentence. A heavy silence drops in the room. Even Janet seems to be doing her best to make herself invisible as she moves around the table, gathering empty plates.

"What happened yesterday was regrettable..." Mrs Allander starts, raising her hand when I open my mouth. "But it can be solved. I believe a letter of apology to Lady Cuttingham is in order."

The very thought disgusts me, but after what Alma said yesterday, I know the choice isn't mine to make.

"Sure," I say simply. "And a letter is probably better than me showing my face at her house."

"Indeed, I believe it is best you restrain... showing your face there for some time," Mrs Allander agrees. "However, you are most welcome to join us for next week's ball in the village. We only have to ensure that you and her Ladyship do not cross paths."

My relief drains away.

"A ball? It would probably be easier if I stayed here?" I say uneasily. "I'm sure Janet could use the help. Or at least the company?"

Hoping for her support, I stare at Janet. But once her back is to Mrs Allander, she smiles widely at me.

"Oh, Miss Max, never!" she exclaims. "I wouldn't want to be the reason why you miss such a dignified evening."

"Traitor," I mutter so that only she can hear me before she leaves the room chuckling, heavy tray in hand.

"It is decided then," Mrs Allander concludes, clasping her hands. "Alma, we must think—"

The sound of the front door opening and closing interrupts her then. We all turn as one, surprised and confused by such an early visit.

Janet runs back into the room, breathless but smiling.

"Ma'am! It is—"

"Please tell me there are eggs left? I am absolutely starving."

A young woman about my age enters the room, wearing a travel dress and a hat in a dark claret colour. Setting down the round box she's carrying, she looks around the table, stopping on each face with a tender expression. It falters only a second when she reaches me.

"Ann!" Alice exclaims once she gets over her shock, throwing herself at the new arrival.

"We did not know you were to be home so soon!" Alma says brightly, joining them and taking the woman's hands in hers.

"My dear, what a joy it is to see you!" Mrs Allander adds, getting up from her seat and opening her arms.

The woman—Ann—walks past me on her way to her mother's embrace, barely sparing me a glance, yet my lungs seem to have stopped working. I turn to follow her movements, my eyes stuck on her face, on her hands.

It's her. The woman from the painting.

Chapter Twelve

And it quickly becomes apparent that she's not a fan of mine.

Once the general shock subsides, we sit back around the table, Alma moving down a seat so that her sister can be closer to their mother. Alice steals my place, leaning forward on the table as she drinks every word coming out of Ann's mouth.

And there are a lot of words.

The retelling of months of social visits and tea parties, card games and travels in carriages. Public balls and private events, dresses, haircuts, ribbons. Rumours and news, who flirted with who, who got engaged to who... It feels endless.

And deeply boring.

Sitting back in my chair, arms crossed, I study her face and her gestures, trying to detect anything that could clarify the whole painting situation. With long brown hair elegantly coiffed, her eyes a dark shade of hazelnut, clear skin and a certain look of intelligence, she's beautiful, yes, I'm not blind. But so are the other women of the house. So why her specifically? What happens that we end up on that painting together?

Meanwhile, her monologue goes on and on.

She barely gratified me with a look or a word since her arrival in the room, instead acting as if I wasn't here. Which is why I'm so startled when she finally turns her gaze on me, meeting mine straight on.

"You must be the famous Max," she says with a neutral smile, tilting her head to look at me. "My apologies, I have been most impolite. My pleasure at being reunited with my family took over me. I should have introduced myself earlier. My name is Ann Allander."

"Max Jones. Mine's Max Jones," I mumble clumsily.

"Pleasure. Your name appeared so often in my sisters' letters that I feel I know you already."

A little worried, I glance at Alma, who nods as if to reassure me about the content of those letters.

"I'm hoping it wasn't to insult me, but well. Your family has been kind enough to take me in, so I wouldn't hold it against them if it were," I try to joke weakly.

"I am sure you have returned this kindness," Ann says.

I feel myself blushing under her stare because somehow, I know she guessed I messed up.

"I, er. I worked in the garden a lot," I attempt, as if it was enough to redeem myself. "And I learned to make pies?"

Alice chuckles next to me.

"The old Mrs Johnson choked on Max's pie when she came for tea," she denounces me.

While Ann seems shocked, Mrs Allander laughs as well.

"Oh, it was quite an afternoon you missed, dear Ann. I believe our disgruntled neighbour will not impose on us any time soon!"

"Mother!" Ann exclaims, now baffled.

"You must agree that tea in her company can be a tiresome experience," Mrs Allander says, gratifying me with a too rare grin. "Max only... added a little entertainment to the afternoon."

"So it seems…" Ann answers, studying me with a frown that makes me look down at the table.

"Oh, but Mother," Alma says suddenly. "Whatever shall we do about the rooms? Now that Ann has returned, where will Max sleep?"

***

"I shall fetch fresh bed sheets, Miss," Janet says from the corridor.

When Ann opens her bedroom door, Janet tries to catch a glimpse of the inside, but I shake my head and wink at her. She sighs and leaves.

Ann thanks her distractedly, not noticing the maid is already gone, before entering her room. I give her a few seconds head start, then follow. As soon as I come in, her neutral expression drops. She closes the door a little too forcibly, putting herself between me and the exit.

"I do not know who you are exactly, but know that I do not trust you."

Her tone is sharp enough to sting, but I do my best not to show it. Turning my back to her, I sit on the edge of the bed, arms stretched behind me.

"Your mother and sisters do. Does it mean you don't trust their judgement?"

"You have appeared one day out of nowhere and seem to have weaselled your way into my family," Ann continues, as if I didn't speak. "Suddenly, my sisters' letters were full of you—"

"Oh, so you're just jealous, then?" I ask with a smirk.

Ann stares at me a little longer, in silence.

"Are you ever serious?"

"I tend to use humour to deflect situations in which I don't feel in control. Or so I've been told," I explain with a shrug.

She freezes.

"Not in control? Whatever do you mean?"

"Well, Ann, it's easy," I say, resting my hands on my skirts to stop fidgeting. "I'm here at the good will of your family, which has worked pretty well for me for the past few weeks. But now, you're here. So my situation is yet again unsettled."

And there's also the fact that we're somehow bound by a magical painting, but I restrain from adding that. I doubt it would make her trust me more.

Ann goes silent again and looks fixedly at me as if she expects to find something on my face. The attention makes me even more uncomfortable.

"The thing is," I start again, "I know you want to throw me out. But I don't think your mother—nor Alma, Alice or Janet for that matter—would be okay with that. We got pretty close when you weren't around."

More silent staring. I sigh.

"Okay, what?"

"Why do you speak in such a manner?" she asks, frowning.

"What do you mean?"

"Your sentences... They always feel shortened and rushed. I do not understand some words you use, and yet, it all seems to come naturally to you."

"Ah yes, that," I say, a little exasperated by the change of subject. "Raised abroad, blabla, mannish habits, blabla, weird manner of speaking. We went over that like, three weeks ago."

That does not relieve the tension on her face.

"You confuse and worry me," she says finally. "The thought of a person as strange as you seem to be around my family does not please me. And let us not forget that regrettable affair with the Cuttinghams. My mother told me."

"That guy is an idiot. The old witch isn't great either, and your sister deserves better. If you don't think so, maybe I'm the one who should be concerned about you," I say defiantly.

Ann looks away and move to grab her travel cloak, settling it gently on the chair facing the desk. Her back turned to me, she smooths the material. A long moment goes by before she speaks again.

"I cannot bring myself to trust you," she says, looking straight at me once more. "But I know my mother and sisters would not agree with me forcing you to leave."

My victorious smile vanishes at her next words.

"However, I know from my mother that you are searching for a way to return... wherever it is you come from."

I can only nod, the mystery of the painting clear in my head.

"So I will not share my suspicions with my family if you agree to act as expected for the reminder of your stay with us. And to not ruin any more prospects for my sister and I."

"Again, I—"

"Not that I disagree with you," she adds with a sigh. "M. Cuttingham is not of the intellectual kind."

"What, an insult!" I exclaim, gaping at her, one hand on my heart. "Have I already tainted you as well?"

She answers with a blank stare.

"Okay, too soon for jokes," I say with regret, raising both hands. "But, hm..."

I look around the room. The clothes I have been given are spread all over, unread books piled on the desk, bedsheets a mess. Good thing I never let Janet in; she would have had a heart attack.

"Where am I going to sleep then?"

Ann goes to the window, picking up an abandoned chemise on the floor with a sour expression.

"The easiest would be for you to remain in another bedroom till the end of your stay with us. However, as you must know, we do not have a spare one. If the choice was mine, I would have you sleep in the attic of the barn, I hear it is quite warm in the summer."

"Ha. Ha."

"But that would attract questions..." she says, pacing as she thinks. "As would your staying with Janet or sleeping in the parlour."

"I can share with Alice. I'm sure she'd be fine with it. She adores me," I say with a smirk, hoping to make her jealous again.

"Do you truly believe I would let a stranger sleep in my little sister's room?"

"To the rest of them, I'm not a stranger," I correct her sharply. "They actually like me. Enough not to imply I'm an absolute weirdo."

Ann ignores me.

"I will sleep in Alma's room," she decides.

But as she says it, I can see it's not an option she's very fond of.

"Why did you grimace?" I ask.

"A lady does not grimace."

"Sure. But you did anyway. Turns out you might be human after all."

With a scoff, she turns away to straighten up a pile of books, then mutters something I don't catch.

"What was that?"

"Alma snores and kicks when she sleeps," Ann repeats much louder, clearly annoyed at having to reveal her sister's habit.

"I see..."

Once I manage to smother my amusement, I stand up, hands clasped.

"Well, it seems there's only one decent option then..."

Which is how later that night, I find myself in bed with a woman who dislikes me very much and to whom I am inexplicably connected, cocooned in my separate bed sheets as she tries to put as much distance as possible between us.

Things are going wonderfully.

Chapter Thirteen

True to her word, Ann keeps her doubts to herself. But I can feel her eyes on me when we're in the same room, her suspicion increasing every time I do or say something. While I understand why she feels that way, it becomes very annoying, very quickly.

But it's not just that.

Before she arrived, I felt like I had found a balance in this situation I was in. I had a clear goal: understanding how and why I was here. My hopes rested on the woman from the painting, because obviously, from the moment I would see her, everything would make sense. She would be seduced by my boldness and my rough charm, and I would learn to appreciate her... whatever.

But because my life is a confusing mess, Ann had to throw me off balance. Nothing happened when I first saw her, except surprise. No tingle or shortness of breath or sudden desire to throw myself at her feet. Once the initial shock passed, I was left with only a slight curiosity and some mild irritation. And in the couple of days since, that annoyance went up a notch as she made sure to remind me that I didn't belong, that I was different.

But the fact remains that somehow we are linked. Will be linked. Or have to be? The answer feels further out of reach than ever.

"You aren't trying!" Ann says exasperatedly as I step to the right instead of the left once again.

"I'm doing my best," I grumble back.

We have been at this for hours. My brain gave up on me ages ago and now it's my body's turn to revolt.

"It really is quite simple," Ann insists, getting up from her chair and pushing me out of the way.

"Ann..." Alma says, worried when she sees me tumbling on my tired legs.

Her sister only grabs her opposite hand and starts counting.

"One, two, three and a turn... Then one, two, three and another turn. See! Simple as day!"

I go lay on the couch to rest my aching feet and ignore her comment, instead rubbing my temples. That woman is a headache personified.

"Would you *please* be kind enough to get up and try once more?" Ann says with a painfully fake smile.

"Would you *please* be kind enough to let me rest for a damn second?" I shoot back, mimicking her annoyingly perfect pronunciation.

"We do not have time to rest! The ball is but in a few days, and you need to be prepared to dance properly when asked!"

"I don't see any reason why anyone would ask me to dance, and even less one to accept!"

Alma goes to sit with Alice by the empty chimney to observe our argument as if it were a tennis match, both heads following each counterattack.

"You promised to obey our rules while you were here!" Ann says.

"And I am! I'm doing your stupid lady lessons. I learned to make polite and meaningless conversation. I even learned the names of your neighbours and I really don't care about any of them! What more do you want?"

"That you learn to dance!"

"I hate dancing!"

"It is not a question of whether you like it or not, I am ordering you to!

That does it. I jump to my feet and step close to her, my face burning.

"You won't force me to do anything. I am my own person."

"Not while you are under our roof," she snarls back.

I hold her angry gaze longer, refusing to back down. But her words pierce into my brain, yet another reminder of my situation. I take a step back.

"You know what? I'm done for today. Leave me alone."

Stomping towards the front door, I ignore Alma's call to at least take a shawl, and disappear down the path leading to the forest.

One of the times I returned to the field to try and figure out anything at all, I marked the spot where I came to with a small pile of stones. I was certain that it meant something. All those weeks later, I'm not so sure anymore.

Once again, I look around morosely, moving a few rocks with my feet, crouching to rip a thin branch out of the ground. And again, there is simply nothing here.

I sit down heavily, legs wide open as if I were wearing my beloved jeans, and lean back on my hands, face tilted towards the sky. Despite everything else, the silence is nice. It's impossible to get that sort of quietness in the city. The rush against time, the endless unsatisfaction, the constant need for more... None of that seems to exist here, at least not to the extent I'm used to.

But suddenly, I miss it all. Being free of being my own person, being allowed to be loud and exuberant and proud. Trying to fit in to what's expected from a woman now makes me feel like a shadow of myself. And Ann's constant nagging doesn't do wonder for my self-esteem and this new-found homesickness.

Not long enough passes before I hear someone approaching. Ann stops in front of me, hands on her hips, blocking the sun from warming my face.

"Do you mind?" I snap.

"Are you—" she starts coldly before audibly forcing herself to sound nicer. "Would you please return to the parlour so that we can continue with the lesson?"

I squint at her before looking away, uninterested.

"Nah. I said I was done for today."

I wave at her to move and close my eyes again when she does, the warmth of the sunshine returning. Her sigh betrays her annoyance, but I couldn't care less. I'm waiting for her to leave, relishing the thought of having a couple of hours to myself, maybe. But to my surprise, she sits down by me, elegantly, of course.

"Alice told me this is where she found you on that first day," she says in a quiet voice. "That you sometimes come back."

"Look who's not making full sentences anymore."

As often, Ann chooses to ignore me.

"Why did you arrive here, in this place?"

"I don't know," I say truthfully.

"How did you arrive here?"

I shrug lamely.

"You must know something, anything," she says, a little impatiently.

I turn my head to look at her. How simple would it be to tell her the whole truth? That for some reason and whether she likes it or not, she's the reason I'm stuck here when I could be in the 21st century, living my own life.

I hold back a sad smile. She wouldn't understand. And being thrown in jail for witchcraft would put a definitive halt on said life.

"I don't," I say finally. "But I'm here for now until I figure out a way back..."

A pressure I didn't realise I felt until now gets to me, and tears form in my eyes. I groan before wiping them with the back of my hand, annoyed. Ann opens her mouth, but I'm faster.

"I know you don't like me or trust me. I know you think I'm not good enough for your family, but I have nowhere else to go. And it's depressing, and it sucks because right now, I'd rather be anywhere than here being constantly criticised and belittled by you. But there's... nothing I can do," I finish in a low voice, disgusted by this simple truth. "So don't make me leave. Please."

"I wouldn't make you leave!" she answers readily.

Looking surprised by her own words, Ann clears her throat before starting again, in a calmer voice.

"Not only because my mother and sisters wouldn't let me, but because I would never leave anyone in distress alone."

"I'm not in distress," I protest.

"Anyone who is in a difficult situation and requires help and assistance, then," Ann says with a too rare smile.

I scoff, but she keeps going.

"Alma told me that perhaps I was being a little... extreme with you," she says, wincing in a quite unladylike manner. "And I am afraid there is some truth to that. So I would like to apologise. To you."

Sitting straighter, I nod at her to continue, my interest awakened. She sighs, but I think I can see a subtle grin appearing at the corner of her lips.

"I know it isn't your fault you aren't familiar with our customs, and that they may not appear as simple to you as they did to us when we were children..."

"Hey!"

"But," she continues, "I have no right to criticise you for shortcomings that, considering your situation, are entirely acceptable. So once more... Please accept my apologies."

I take a moment to digest that.

"If we omit the barely hidden insults, I guess that was a decent apology."

"Yes. It seems I am human after all," Ann concludes, making me chuckle unexpectedly.

However, my amusement dissolves with a sigh at the thought of going back inside.

"Do I really have to learn to dance?" I almost whimper. "I can't do it and it's a waste of everyone's time."

Ann thinks for a second, tapping her fingers against her leg.

"One dance," she says. "If you accept to try and master one dance, I promise I will find excuses for you to avoid the other dances."

I look at her, suspicious.

"Why does it feel like a trap? Are you also going to tell people I have a head injury?"

"A head injury?" she says, surprised. "What on earth—"

"Eh, ask your sister," I reply before pausing to think. "Okay. Deal. One dance."

She gets up first, shaking her skirt to dislodge the strands of grass, before reaching for me.

"One dance," she promises as I let her haul me up.

We walk back to the house in silence until Ann breaks it.

"You miss your home, do you not?"

I should say yes. That's the answer that seems logical. Expected. But as I think back on my life with the Allanders before Ann arrived, that's not the one I want to say. So I settle for a neutral reply, and the words come out quieter than I hoped.

"Something like that."

Chapter Fourteen

Despite my previous reluctance, we do finish the dance lesson without another incident. It turns out I learn better when I'm not being shouted at. Ann takes a step back for the rest of it, letting Alma lead and even contributing one or two helpful comments. Surprisingly, it becomes fun, just a little.

After that, we move on to our respective chores for the day. Ann and Alma help Janet in the kitchen; Mrs Allander and Alice dust the rooms; I disappear into the garden.

I get to work gladly, happy to dirty my hands and to have a moment to think on my own. But too soon, my back starts to hurt from me leaning forward, so, after throwing a glance around to ensure I'm alone, I knot the hem of the skirts mid-thigh, and kneel to pull on an obstinate dead potato plant. I must have used a little too much force, however, because I tumble on my back with a surprised cry. Then immediately burst out laughing. My hair and the back of my dress are most probably covered in dry mud, but I stay down anyway, looking up at the clear sky, chest heaving.

"Max? Dinner!" Alma's voice floats to me through the back door.

I take a deep breath before getting up, then make my way back to the house with a satisfied smile, rubbing at the stains on my skirt to remove the worst of the dirt.

"Why do I feel like such a state will be a regular occurrence with you?" Ann says from where she's leaning against the wall inside, something unexpected on her face: she looks amused.

"It was simpler that way," I shrug.

I twist to dust the back of my bare legs before fussing to remove the knot in my skirts. Stepping outside again for a second, I shake my hair and dress. When I look up, Ann's face seems a little flushed, but she ignores my curious glance and immediately disappears into another room without another word.

Okay then.

Entering the dining room after her, I find Alice and Alma already seated and steal Alice's bun on the way to my own chair.

"My bread!" she exclaims.

"I believe you mean *my* bread," I tease her, taking a large bite.

"I will get your dessert for that!" she threatens.

"I dare you."

Mrs Allander joins us, placing down a plate of boiled potatoes in the middle of the table. She asks before even sitting down,

"Are your lessons going well, Max?"

"Oh, it's, er, fine. I think?" I hesitate, glancing at Alma for support.

"It is all going very well, Mother. Max is a most dedicated student," she adds kindly.

"Wonderful. I believe we can all look forward to the ball, then."

"There is still much work to be done," Ann adds, her voice a little too sharp for my taste.

I sigh, exasperated.

"Alma says I'm doing fine. So it's fine."

"I wouldn't be too certain," Ann mutters haughtily before pouring a glass of wine for her mother.

I squint at her but drop it, instead focusing on Alice's "stealth" attempts to pick on my plate.

***

I close the bedroom door none too gently behind me and throw the book I have been pretending to read for the past couple of hours on the bed. It bounces and falls on the floor, but I don't even rush to pick it up. That's how annoyed I am.

"Ok, what's your problem now?" I snarl. "First, you're suspicious towards me, which I can understand. But then you're sort of nice and helpful, then you get all mean again? Can you please make up your mind? I feel like I'm collecting migraines."

"I am not sure what you mean," Ann says, her back turned to me as she lets down her hair for the night.

"I thought we had a deal and that you understood I was trying really hard. But then, you criticise me again during dinner? What more can I do, seriously?"

"I did not mean to criticise you. I only stated a fact," she adds in a calm voice.

I pause for a second, waiting for her to say something more.

"Okay, whatever," I say when she doesn't. "Have it your way."

Stomping around the room, I get rid of my dirty dress and my chemise to put on the frilly nightdress I somewhat got used to. I shiver a little when the cold air hits my skin.

"What are you—" Ann exclaims in an unnaturally shrill voice.

I finish adjusting the nightdress before turning to her.

"What?"

"Could you not—Why would you—" she sputters.

It takes me a second to understand what seems to have broken her.

"You don't have to look, you know?" I smirk at her.

"You—"

"Changing elsewhere every night was a favour to you. But as you're not making any effort towards me, I won't either. Also, it's cold outside the room at night and I'm not a fan of that. So get used to it," I declare before wrapping myself in my bedsheets and turning my back to her side of the room.

She does not speak for a long time, nothing but the sound of her brush filling the silence. When she finally comes to bed, it feels like the space she leaves between us is wider than ever.

"Why do you have those on your arms?" she asks, apparently aware I'm not asleep. "Those drawings."

I try to remember every detail of the story I told the others, but too much has happened since. It's all a little blurry.

"I, er. When I was in Canada, I met sailors that had—"

"What is the real reason?" she interrupts.

"Ah. Well. I... like them."

Laying on my back, I raise my sleeves to my elbows and rotate my forearms slowly.

"They all have meaning to me, and for most, I've done them at particular times of my life that I wanted commemorated."

She studies the marks on my skin for a moment, the flicker of the candle brushing her face with red and yellow.

"What is the meaning of this one?" she asks, pointing at three keys hanging from a ribbon.

"This was..." I start, trying to find the words to make it 19th century-friendly. "Those were the keys to my first home."

I can't explain the whole story of what this place meant to me. That it was my first real flat and where I met the people who became my best friends then. Where I realised who I was and where I wanted to stand in the world as a queer person.

"And this?" Ann says, turning my arm a little to reveal flowers intertwined.

"Those represent cities that matter a lot to me," I explain, pointing at each flower in turn. "London here, then New York. And Kyoto here. That's in Japan."

She looks at me with wonder then, an expression I decide here and now I would like to see again.

"You have travelled the world..." she says, envy clear in her voice.

"I was... lucky," I answer, realising only now how true that is.

Ann moves on to my second arm, leaning forward and twisting it slightly towards her. It's an uncomfortable position for me, but she seems too focused to mind.

"What of this one?" she says, passing her finger lightly on a cursive inscription below the crook of my elbow.

When her eyes meet mine, we both realise how much closer this new position brought us and she lets go of my arm. But she doesn't move back.

"It's a quote. From a book," I manage to say, finding myself unexpectedly a little out of breath.

"*My queerness is not a vice, is not deliberate, and harms no one*," she reads, following the lines with the tip of her finger before frowning. "I do not understand. What does it mean?"

I chastise myself mentally, almost regretting not getting a more subtle quote tattooed in case I ever found myself transported to the 19th century.

"It means, er... There is a part of me—a large part of me—that is, hm..." I fail miserably to explain before clearing my throat. "It means that the part of me that differentiates me from... others isn't bad and shouldn't be treated as such."

"The part that differentiates you..." she whispers back.

Her mind visibly elsewhere, she caresses my tattoo again, fingers light on my skin. Then her eyes meet mine.

She jerks back away from me, covering herself with her bed sheets up to her chin. Assuming the exploration is over, I roll down my sleeves and meet her gaze with an amused smile.

"Any more questions?"

"Good night," she replies in a strangled voice.

Ann turns to face the other side of the room and disappears under her cover. Wondering, I look at her a little longer, then lay more comfortably on my back, unreachable questions floating in my mind.

Chapter Fifteen

The rest of the week goes quietly. Once I have more or less mastered the required dance, I spend most of my days with Alma and Alice as they help with my final lessons. Ann stays away, our interactions once again limited to a bare minimum since our tattoo talk. Which makes the evenings quite awkward.

But when the last night before the ball arrives, I find myself worrying an obscene amount.

"Wouldn't it be better if I stayed here, really?" I beg, following Mrs Allander as she goes from room to room. "Imagine if I make a mistake or say something stupid and shame your whole family!"

She hums softly in response.

"Or what if I somehow set the place on fire or pour wine on someone important or something?"

"I hardly believe this could happen," is her only answer.

"I can be really clumsy though! Honestly, I should stay here and then you can tell me all about it when you're back. I'm sure it's going to be fasci—"

Mrs Allander suddenly stops in front of a low commode in the south corridor. She opens it and all but throws at me the layers of light dresses and scarves resting on top. I manage to catch them at the last minute in a bundle of floaty fabric.

"—nating," I finish, thin fringes tickling my face.

"Ah. There it is," she says, sounding pleased.

Carefully, she unwraps the package in her hands and unfolds its content before turning to me. Looking more closely, I see a delicate wrap, wildflowers sewn in shades of red, blue and lilac, the colours contrasting with the ivory fabric. Mrs Allander lays it on my shoulders, answering my confusion with a kind smile.

"This is for you to wear to the ball," she explains. "It is a tradition in our family that mothers present an item of theirs to their daughters before their first ball."

"But I'm not—" I say, frowning.

"Perhaps. Yet I know you will make me proud tomorrow night, just like a daughter would."

I caress the fabric covering my shoulders, lingering on the soft threads, words seeming insufficient.

"It looks lovely on you, dear," she adds before pressing a light kiss on my forehead, one hand on my cheek.

She disappears at the turn of the corridor, leaving me to drown in emotions I don't quite understand.

***

Holding the wrap tightly to my chest, I enter Ann's room and drop on the bed, needing to make sense of those feelings. I pass my hands on the fabric, exploring its softness and the contrasting texture of the threads, then press it to my cheek, eyes closed.

Why would Mrs Allander give such a precious gift to me? Is it her way to bribe me so that I behave tomorrow? But if she were that worried, why not just let me stay at the house? Wouldn't it be simpler for everyone that way?

But no, it can't be that. I may not have known her for long, but it has been long enough to be convinced she wouldn't lie or cheat. And her smile, her words. Her hand resting on my cheek... I shake my head, trying to refocus on a more plausible reason.

I didn't realise I wasn't alone in the room until someone steps too close, startling me.

"Are you unwell?" Ann asks with the air of someone who repeated themselves already.

"What? No. No, I'm fine," I answer distractedly, moving the fabric in my hands.

"Ah, I see Mother gave you her present. Good," she says before returning to the half-written letter on her desk.

"You mean you knew about it?" I ask, my suspicions rising again.

"Of course. She spoke of it to me yesterday. I advised her it was a good idea."

"Did you now."

I start pacing around the room, the wrap crushed in my tight fist. Ann looks up at me.

"What's your goal here?" I ask her coldly. "It takes more than a piece of fabric to make me act the way you want, you know."

She frowns, her mouth a fine line.

"I am afraid I do not know what you mean."

"You told your mum to give me this scarf, didn't you? So that I would feel trusted and part of the family. So that I would think it's my duty to be on my best behaviour."

When she doesn't answer, I let my anger explode.

"That was so unnecessary! I'm going to do my best during this damn ball because your family has been kind to me, not because of your little games. I may have whined and complained, but I never had any intention of messing things up for any of them. I can't believe you manipulated your own mother!"

"Is this really what you think of me?"

"What else am I supposed to think? You say you don't trust me, then you start acting nice, then you ignore me, and then you do such a stupid thing behind my back! What's your problem with me, seriously? Say it and let's be done with it!"

"My problem with you?" she whispers, standing up, her face crimson. "Apart from the fact that you appeared out of nowhere and completely unsettled our lives? That my sisters, even my mother, are deeply fond of you despite you doing *nothing* to deserve it? You even lied about who you are and where you come from! I have to share my own room and bed with you. I have to lie next to you each night knowing—"

"Knowing?" I insist, curiosity mixing with my anger as Ann seems to be debating within herself. "Knowing what?"

"Nothing," she snaps, raising her chin haughtily. "But know that you are wrong. I have not manipulated my mother, nor am I acting in the way you described. I am only trying to... understand."

"Understand what?"

"Well, you."

I stare at her, unsettled.

"And what does that mean, exactly?"

"Ever since we met, you seem to have been expecting something from me, although you never said a word," she says, studying the change in my expression. "I know you are hiding something from me, something important. And I would like to know what it is."

Ignoring my surprise, she goes to open the box at the end of her bed and takes out some very familiar clothing.

"According to my sisters, this is what you were wearing when you arrived."

She drops my jeans, shirt and boots on the bed.

"While I may not have travelled as extensively as you did, I am cultured enough to know that nowhere in the known world, those are worn by ladies. So..."

She takes a step back, her defiant stance contrasting with the eagerness of her expression.

"Who are you, and where did you come from?"

Chapter Sixteen

"I, hm..."

"I have known you to be more eloquent," Ann remarks, looking down at where I'm sitting on the bed.

I stare at the floor, thoughts crashing into each other in a mad frenzy as I try to figure out a way out of this.

"I told your mother and—"

"I know very well what you told them. I also know that, like me, they do not believe your story. However, they chose not to press the matter. I do not."

"Why can't you just believe it?"

"Because while improbable, your story seems too simple for all that you are."

"Er... Thank you?"

She doesn't answer, crossing her arms tighter against her chest and staring at me with clear impatience.

"What if I just didn't tell you?" I ask with a sigh. "You promised me I could stay here if I didn't ruin things for you guys, and I haven't since. So good luck explaining why you want to force me out to your mum and sisters."

She seems taken aback by that, as if she didn't explore the possibility I would flatly refuse to speak.

"You are asking me to keep a promise I made to you. So you have to have trust in me to be certain I will not break it," she says finally. "Let me have trust in you too."

The disarming honesty of her tone makes me hesitate a second. Just enough for the possible consequences of my real story to catch up to me. Yet... Ann is the key to this whole mystery. What if telling her who I am is how I can get closer to going back to my own time? What if this secret is what held me back all these weeks? What if I could turn this to my advantage...

But before I can say anything, there's a knock on the door and I rush to open it, relieved not to have to decide immediately. Finding Alma there, she seems surprised by my eagerness.

"Do you need me to do something elsewhere? You do, right?" I ask, already halfway in the corridor.

"Well, I—"

"Tell me on the way!" I say, pushing her towards the staircase.

"Max, no! It is my sister I came to see," she exclaims.

"Even better. Keep her busy for as long as you want, please, thank you," I plead, making my way downstairs before any of them can speak another word.

I'm relieved to find Alice in the parlour, reading with Fitz by her side. She makes space for me on the couch, and I try to get the cat to settle on my lap, which he does by repeatedly planting his claws in my thigh.

Alice and I read together, switching voices for each character, until she falls asleep. As quietly as possible, I help her upstairs to her bed, then return to the parlour to make myself a nest of cushions and blankets, wondering what to do next.

***

I manage to avoid Ann for most of the following day, for which I have the ball preparations to thank. As the afternoon brings us closer to the fateful hour, Janet barely gives me a second to breathe. She spins around me, making final adjustments to the stiff, long-sleeved navy dress I'm forced to wear, and worries about being unable to tame my short hair.

When Alice pops into the room at some point, she bursts out laughing when she sees the army of ribbons Janet used to try to make me presentable. I immediately take them all off, ready to deal with Janet's annoyance. Instead, when she turns to me, it's resignation she shows.

"Yes, it is perhaps better this way..." she regrets, collecting the fallen ribbons.

"Look, I'll just..."

Tilting my head back, I gather my hair the best I can, then grab a piece of white cloth to make some sort of bun. I take a look at myself in the mirror.

"It isn't what I would have liked, but it will have to do," Janet sighs.

Once that's done, she asks me to stand straight and to put on my shoes. She takes a turn around me, looking closely to find a last-minute imperfection. Seeing my reflection in the mirror, I can spot more than one, but I don't utter a word.

"You are ready," she announces finally.

After adjusting the flowery wrap on my shoulders, Janet gestures to the door, her attention already turned elsewhere.

"Please join Mrs Allander downstairs. I believe she is waiting for you. I will see if the Misses need help..."

"Hey Janet," I say before she leaves the room. "Thank you."

She looks at me with her kind eyes opened wide and blushes before making her exit. With her gone, I take one last look at myself, flatten the skirt of my dress, and sigh.

"Let's do this, I guess."

***

Mrs Allander is indeed waiting for me downstairs, ready to leave. Her face relaxes when she sees me.

"Did you expect a disaster?"

"Of course not," she answers with a teasing smile. "Only a minor catastrophe, perhaps."

I quickly forget my snarky reply when Alma and Ann come down the stairs. Alma is lovely as always, flowers threading the crown of hair wrapped around her head. Her dress seems light and floaty, and even though I know it's the same fabric as mine, the effect is different on her. Her face is turned towards Ann in a laugh, and when my eyes follow her movement, I gasp a little.

If Alma is lovely, Ann is resplendent. The dark yellow of her dress matches perfectly the brown hair that curls against her forehead and ears. A simple necklace rests on her collarbones, bringing attention to a zone below her jaw that I would love to—

I frown at the thought and clear my throat, my voice coming out strangled, anyway.

"Hey ladies, looking nice tonight!"

Then I immediately cringe and turn red, covering my face with both hands when Alma laughs.

"A wonderful compliment, I am sure," she says, touching my shoulder as she reaches my side. "Mother, shall we depart?"

Ann stops on the last step, her gaze fixed on me. I struggle to meet it, instead focusing on Alice who walks past us, head low.

"I wish I could come..." she says.

"Oh, it won't be that great, you know..." I answer, a little sorry to see her sad expression.

Which, worryingly, brightens as soon as I speak.

"How could that be? It is your first ball, it will be chaos!"

I burst out laughing while Mrs Allander chastises her youngest.

"Alice! Nothing unseemly will happen tonight! Girls, come now," she orders, leading us towards the door.

I have just the time to wink at Alice, making her giggle, before the door is closed and we're herded into a carriage.

Chapter Seventeen

As we arrive at the ball, I can see three major issues rising. First, I need to do whatever I can to avoid Ann tonight. Second, try to not make enemies of anyone important. Or anyone at all, really. And third, do my best to stay upright in those slippery shoes and that stupid long dress that is tight as a binder.

The first should be easy as Ann grabs Alma's arm as soon as we get inside and disappear into another room. Second turns out to be less stressful than expected. Most of the people Mrs Allander introduces me to are quite curious about me, though not to the point of talking to me more. Or asking me to dance. As for Lady Cuttingham, we avoid her when she appears by the musicians, probably telling them how to do their jobs.

I find relief for problem number 3 when, after an hour or so, I catch sight of a chair a little hidden and claim it. I want nothing more than to massage my aching feet but decide against it when I imagine Ann's reaction. Instead, I scan the room.

So far, my experience of the 19th century has been one terrible social visit. After that, I didn't exactly leave the house, even to go to the village, and I didn't mind. The Allanders were more than enough to keep me busy. Maybe that's why it hits me so hard now, as I look around the room, how far I am from everything I know. It feels like

I have stumbled into a period drama, and I have to keep reminding myself that it's the real thing. That I'm the one who's out of place.

I catch a few curious glances my way, but ignore them, instead focusing on Alma dancing with a young man, not for the first time of the evening, I think. Maybe. All those guys look the same to me. Her movements are graceful and natural. She seems to be having fun, which helps me discard my unhappy thoughts.

Ann also stands on the dancefloor, a few couples away from her sister, displaying the complete opposite of Alma's relaxed expression. Her face couldn't be more tense, her movements more forced. And yet, she's still beautiful...

I jerk back on my chair when her dark eyes meet mine and immediately look down, a little worried to have been caught staring. But I can't help it. And when I glance at her again, her gaze is still on me, which awakens a little thrill that shouldn't be here.

We keep staring at each other, the contact only breaking when she twirls or changes sides. I can't seem to be able to look away. Curls of her hair escape to fly around her cheeks, reddened by the dance. The folds of her dress moving with her hypnotize me. Her expression doesn't waver for a second, her gaze holding mine.

Then, the music stops. She barely gratifies her partner with a final look before she starts in my direction. Only to be stopped by another man bowing and probably asking for the next dance. By then, I have already jumped from my chair and begun to make my way through the crowd before she can catch me.

Finding a man in a red uniform holding a tray of glasses, I grab one and down it thankfully before wiping my mouth with the back of my hand. Realising too late that it isn't quite ladylike, I freeze for a second before smiling tightly at the man and curtsying, frantically planning my escape. But before I'm able to run away, he hands the tray to a man from his group, then bows, one arm folded behind his back.

"Please forgive my impertinence, Miss, for we have not been formally introduced, but I would be most pleased to know your name, if you would do me the honour."

I look around, unsure of what to do.

"Er. Max. Max Jones."

"Officer Danes at your service, Miss Jones. I am delighted to make your acquaintance," he says with a too bright smile. "Would you accept my hand... for the next dance?"

Barely holding back a wince at this poor flirting attempt, I panic when I see Ann making her way through the crowd. She pauses when her eyes find me.

"Yes. Dancing. Awesome. Let's go now," I say, dragging the man towards the dancefloor by the sleeve.

A little too late, a problem makes its way into my mind as we stand amongst the couples chatting and laughing...

I only know one dance.

From what Alma explained, there's a 95% chance I have not learned this one. Panic takes hold as the music starts and everyone exchange bows, which I remember to do only a second too late.

Despite everything, relief washes over me when I see Ann making her way to the dancefloor, accompanied by a random man. She settles in the spot next to mine and glances at me before nodding towards her feet and raising her arms halfway. I take it as an order to follow what she's doing.

When paying attention both to her and my partner turns out to be impossible, I cut off the second, answering him only with a nod or a hum. Instead, I focus on copying each of Ann's steps, cursing under my breath when stupid twirls make me lose my concentration.

It feels like an eternity passes before the song finally ends. My partner steps closer and takes my hand in his, dropping a kiss on the back of it.

"Thank you for the dance, Miss Max Jones. It was most refreshing."

"Yes, sure. That," I agree vaguely as Ann probably receives the same meaningless compliment.

Yet again, she turns to where I stand, and our gazes meet. I disappear in a hurry, a testimony of my maturity.

Rushing through the rooms, I eventually find an empty balcony hidden behind a heavy curtain. Relieved to finally be alone, I remember to sit on my heels not to ruin the back of my dress because that would disappoint Janet. I try to run a hand through my hair, remembering too late that it's tied up. So I take off the ribbon, tangled strands brushing my cheeks, and close my eyes, focusing on calming down my breathing.

I can't keep doing this. I can't keep running away from Ann if I want to find a solution to this whole insane situation. She *will* catch me and delaying the inevitable does no good to anyone. So despite how reluctant I am to the idea, I know what needs to be done.

Nonetheless, I stay hidden until I hear the first carriages arrive and Mrs Allander looking for me.

Chapter Eighteen

Alice bursts into the corridor when she hears the door open, and immediately showers me with questions.

"Did anything burn down? Did you duel? Did you spill food or wine on an elderly guest?" she asks eagerly.

"Sadly enough for you, it all went fine," I reply, more than a little tired. I'm still avoiding everyone's eyes. And by everyone, I mean Ann. "I think I'll go to bed though, if that's ok."

"But—" Alice protests.

"Come, dear, we will tell you everything," Mrs Allander says to her youngest. "But first, would you be kind enough to go ask Janet for some tea?"

Not wasting a second, Alice rushes towards the kitchen. Mrs Allander turns to me.

"Thank you for tonight, Max."

"I didn't do much," I mumble. "I mostly hid away."

"Perhaps, but you showed yourself to be polite when it mattered," Alma says. "Even Lady Cuttingham seems to have forgotten all about your first meeting."

I frown.

"Does it mean that you and Boring-ham—"

Alma looks away, a tense smile on her lips that I'm not sure how to read.

"Let us talk more tomorrow," Mrs Allander interrupts. "Good night, Max."

"Night all."

Once in Ann's room upstairs, I lean against the door and allow myself to let out a deep sigh, physically and mentally exhausted. I struggle with my dress for a moment, the lacing just a little out of reach, before managing to take it off by wiggling wildly.

I'm barely wrapped in my bedsheet that the door opens, Ann walking in with a hand against her eyes.

"I'm decent, if that's what you're afraid of," I mock her from the bed.

She drops her hand immediately and glances at the dress abandoned on the back of her chair.

"I was afraid you wouldn't be able to unlace it on your own..."

"So what? You came to see if you could kindly help me? I didn't know we were back to that phase."

"Perhaps you would if you had not avoided me the entire evening," Ann says mildly.

She goes to close the curtains before speaking again, her back still to me.

"Why did you avoid me so?" she asks.

"Why do you think?"

"Are you so afraid of the truth?"

"Not of the truth, but of its consequences."

"What could be so terrible? I doubt you are a criminal or someone I should be afraid of."

"Don't speak too soon."

I drop my head on the pillow and close my eyes, almost wishing Ann would just go away. But when I open them again, she's sitting at the other end of the bed, looking at me insistently.

"Please," she says in a too quiet voice I'm not used to hear from her. "Trust me."

I sigh heavily. Well then. Hoping it won't come crashing down on me, I get out of bed to open the heavy box on Ann's left, taking my modern clothes out of it. My back turned to Ann, I drag the jeans up my legs under my nightdress, then remove the cotton nightmare to put on my shirt, leaving a few buttons opened at the neck. I roll the sleeves up and tuck the hem in my waistband. Finally, I slip on my heavy boots, leaving them unlaced, smiling at the self-confidence I feel at being back in my own clothes.

Turning around, hands in my pockets, I face Ann's puzzled expression.

"This is who I am," I say. "Maximilia Jones, 25 years old, born on April 20th, 1997. Raised in London and still living there, until I found myself transported here on May 29th, 2022."

I give her a second to absorb the information before speaking again.

"How is that for trust?"

Chapter Nineteen

The second night on my improvised parlour nest isn't as pleasant as the first. Maybe because two days ago, it was my choice to avoid Ann. Now it's hers.

After she pushed me out of the room and locked the door, I debated what to do for a long time. I sat in the corridor, hoping she would open and say that she believed me and that funnily enough, Kevin from the neighbouring village came from the 1930s. We would laugh at the wonders of time travel and resume our passive-aggressive relationship, everything else forgotten.

But an hour passed, and the door stayed locked. Eventually, I moved down to the parlour, draping one of the blankets on my shoulders to cover my clothes in case someone came to investigate. I laid on the couch, facing the empty chimney as I tried to figure out what to do now. Nothing came for hours and hours, not even panic, not even relief.

The look on Ann's face after my revelation haunted me. She was frightened of me.

Maybe... Maybe I should return upstairs, tell her it was just a bad joke and that I'm sorry, that she doesn't have to be scared of me. For some reason, I can't stand the idea that she is.

Answering my instinct, I leave my boots by the couch to be as quiet as possible. When I reach her door, I knock gently once, then twice. Then three times. My ear pressed to the wood, I hear Ann moving inside and can easily imagine her frowning face, the tension in her shoulders.

Looking around for an idea, I notice the slight gap under the door, so I return downstairs to look for something to write on, settling for the back of a neighbour's old note. It takes me a few tries to master the pen, spilling more ink than I should, but I doubt Ann will focus on that.

My plead scribbled, I return upstairs once more, lungs complaining at the exercise. I lower myself on my knees, push the folded paper under the gap, and poke it with my finger to make it go all the way. Then I sit in front of the door, passing the time by damaging the skin around my nails as Ann continues to ignore me.

A long moment goes by before I accept that she won't speak to me. I sit against the wall, too tired to even return downstairs, and wrap the blanket more tightly around myself. I lay my head against the cold surface, my eyelids heavy...

And Ann opens the door. I get up in a rush, suddenly wide awake. Ann's defiant expression sends an inexplicable shiver right through me, which vanishes when she raises her candlestick, the flame almost licking my cheek.

"Hey! Careful," I exclaim, jumping back.

She looks both ways, maybe to make sure we're alone, then steps back into the room, her weapon still raised. Taking it as an order to follow, I do just so, closing the door behind me.

"I am armed," she warns unnecessarily.

"Yeah, I'm not blind," I mutter, rubbing my cheek that still feels a little too warm. "You could have hurt me."

She falters at that but toughens her expression.

"What are you?"

"I told you..."

"Your words make no sense. I have been turning them in my mind for hours now, but... You must be lying. Or you must have lost your mind. This is impossible."

"Yet here I am," I say, sitting on the edge of the bed and gesturing vaguely to my whole self.

"You could have stolen those clothes from a man somewhere."

"Why would I steal something that makes me stand out so much?"

"I do not know!" she says, her voice betraying her frustration. "To... To raise pity and make my family care for you!"

"You're the one that doesn't make sense now."

"I am! I..." she says, lowering the candle a little, a wild look on her face. "You came here, lied to my family, earned their trust... But what is your plan, your goal in this?"

I press the talons of my hands against my eyes, sighing heavily.

"There's no plan, okay? No final goal, no hidden intention, no nefarious nothing. I told you: I don't know why exactly I'm here."

"You would have me believe you came here from the... the future," she almost spats, "with no intentions at all?"

"I didn't come here, I woke up here," I correct her. "That's where your argumentation fails. It wasn't my choice."

"But why would you—How can it be that..."

I stand up suddenly, tired of trying to justify the unjustifiable. If I'm going down, I might as well tell her everything I know because I can't stay here, not anymore. And anyway, I should try to go back to, well, my own actual life.

I look around the room, realising sadly that the only things belonging to me are the ones I'm wearing. It will make packing easy, but it won't do for whatever awaits me now.

So, while I try to find the words to explain myself, I pick up a few things I could need, gathering them on the bed. Keeping busy somehow makes it easier to think, even if Ann is still staring at me in silence.

"Okay, I may have kept part of the truth because, well... it's you," I say, attempting a light tone.

Looking up, I meet her confused gaze, so I clarify further.

"You're the reason I'm here."

Ann stumbles as she tries to sit on the chair and ends up crashing into the closest wall, looking even more stunned.

"You're okay?" I ask, reaching for her.

"How—How could that be?" she whispers, eyes wide, not hearing me.

"That's the thing I don't understand," I confess, retreating back to the bed as she doesn't seem to be hurt. "But somehow, you must be the key for me to go back."

"But why me? What could possibly be the reason?"

Though she seems to be coming around to my improbable situation, it's definitively too soon for the possible sapphic aspect of it.

"It seems we became... good friends," I tread carefully. "And that, somehow, me being here has something to do with you."

"No... No!" she says, jumping to her feet, reaching for the candle again.

I study her for a moment, her defensive stance, the lost look on her face, then make myself comfortable against the pillows.

"It's going to be a long night, isn't it..." I sigh.

***

And indeed it is. After I finish explaining the real story behind my arrival here, Ann goes from disbelief and sharp refusal to asking me questions about the future. It goes a little like this.

"You created an evil scheme to steal our house!" she accuses me.

"I agree that prices in London are crazy, but I wouldn't go as far as to time travel to the 19th century to get a house," I snort.

And...

"You say that those... rough breeches are worn by everyone in your time? Women as well as men?" she asks in awe.

"Yup. And you should see in the summer. We wear those, but cut way above our knees, showing most of our legs. Isn't that perfectly indecent?" I tease her.

She frowns like never before.

And again...

"You are a witch. It is the only possible explanation..." Ann says, pacing in circles.

"Yes, you got me," I reply, letting out a yawn. "I'm an evil witch. Fitz is actually my demon cat and we're planning for world domination."

Or...

"Explain it to me again..." she asks from where she's sitting in front of me on the bed.

"Well, it's still quite bad because opportunities are limited by socio-economic issues and—

"Max. Please."

Looking at her, I feel like I've been showering her with fairy tales for the past few hours. Her conflicted expression, split between wonder and apprehension, makes me soften.

"Sure. So basically, everyone that can afford it is allowed an education. Men, women and everyone in between. And though we're still horrifyingly looked down upon and that society is far from being fair, in theory, in most countries, women are allowed to vote. We can dress how we want and say what we want, we can aim for higher education and well-paid positions at work..."

"But what of your husband?"

I snort.

"Husbands are not a necessity, more of a choice. For whoever wants them," I add, trying to spot the impact of my words on her expression.

Ann doesn't seem to notice the attention, however, too distracted by her thoughts.

"It seems like a wonderful time..." she says in a quiet voice.

"In some ways, it can be," I reply slowly. "But it's very far from being even remotely decent."

Her crestfallen look stops me from saying more. We stay silent for a moment, both lost in our own minds. To me, my era is an infinite mess with no solution in sight. But to Ann... To someone who was born to become a wife and nothing more, never even allowed to consider more, who has to depend on a man, whose only education consists of a little reading, music and drawing, but mostly household chores...

"I'm known to be cynical," I start, not sure where I'm going with this, "so I'm hardly the best person to defend my century. But progress has been made since yours, for sure, good progress..."

She looks at me then, head tilted.

"I guess what I'm trying to say is... You shouldn't settle for less than what you deserve. Because women now and later in history are and will fight for more, for what we truly deserve."

"Fight for what we deserve..." she repeats carefully, as if trying out the words.

It goes on and on for a long time until morning announces itself softly through the window. By then, I have relocated under the cover, still wrapped in my blanket like a burrito—which I described to Ann to her amazement. She now sits at the end of the bed, on the wooden box.

"So…" I try hesitantly, my voice rough from talking all night. "Do you believe me now?"

When she gets up and starts pacing again, I'm worried she's going to grab the candlestick once more. But instead, she buries her hands in her hair, brushing it back. I stare.

"I think I do, yes," she says with a sigh. "Despite my better judgment and a sound mind. It would be easier not to. Yet, there are so many things you know…"

"You don't think I made up any of it?"

"It seems impossible that you could imagine such precise and numerous details so rapidly… But…"

Ann stops in the middle of the room, wrapping her arms around herself. Her distress floats to me and I sit up, unable to ignore it.

"I can go, if you need," I say, surprised not to sound more reluctant. "I don't want to create more problems for you and your family."

"And where would you go?" she says, looking almost annoyed. "You have no one else here."

"I don't know, I'll… walk around. Until I find a solution."

"Nonsense!"

Ann clears her throat when I gaze at her curiously.

"Nonsense," she repeats in a calmer voice. "You say I am the reason you are here."

"So it seems."

"Which means you cannot go anywhere I am not."

I hide a smile behind my hand at the blush that appears on her face when she realises what just left her mouth.

"Not till we understand why you are here and how you can go back to your... own time," she adds, looking away.

Obviously, I'm quite happy at not having to disappear in the cold morning without an explanation, but I need to ask.

"Are you sure you're fine with me being here? Now that you know everything?"

Well, almost everything. I try to ignore the sight of her dishevelled appearance. Her long hair let down in a mess on her shoulders, her cheeks still a little reddened, her lids heavy with sleep, and...

"I choose to believe you," she says, her voice determined. "Which means that you depend on me."

"Well, I wouldn't say depend..." I protest weakly.

"According to your own words, I am the "key" to your situation," she says, accentuating the word with a smirk. "So it seems you *will* have to depend on me."

"You're lucky I actually need your help," I mutter rebelliously.

As often, Ann ignores me and instead straightens up, takes a long breath in and clasps her hands.

"Very well. Let us get you home, shall we?

Chapter Twenty

When I wake up in our shared bed some time later, Ann is already halfway to establishing of list of "How did Max get here?". She's sitting on the floor, surrounded by opened books, and currently focused on the large leather-bound volume resting on her lap. When she looks up at the sound of the bedsheets rustling, I catch a glance of the title.

"*English Tales and Folklore*..." I read slowly. "What even—"

"Do not dismiss the idea, not when you were inexplicably transported back in time. Which, to my understanding, rarely occurs. Perhaps there is something to be found in those..." Ann says, waving me off to focus on her reading again.

I pause for a second, wondering if, though far-fetched, there couldn't be an ounce of truth in that. But logic takes over. I get out of bed, shivering as my bare feet touch the floor, then kneel in front of Ann to close the book on her lap.

"I was reading!" she protests.

"Sorry to disappoint, but as far as I know, I'm not a fairy or a gnome."

"Of course not, but—"

"I guess there's a part of magic in all of this, if not a breach in time and space or whatever. But how I came here isn't the answer to *why* I'm here or how I can go back, so..."

"Indeed," Ann says, frowning.

She picks up a piece of paper half covered with slant handwriting.

"Could it be that you have something tying you to our time, then? An ancestor, perhaps?"

Visibly entranced by the idea, she grabs the pen abandoned on the floor and starts scratching fervently. I wave my hand in front of her eyes to catch her attention.

"I told you, Ann. It's for you that I'm here. I don't think there's anyone else."

To my surprise, she blushes vividly.

"Why must you say it this way..."

"Say what?" I frown. "I meant the painting. It's when I touched our painting that it happened."

The serious expression that's more familiar to me returns.

"Describe it to me once more. This painting."

I take a second, as much to think of details I could have forgotten last night, as to make sure I don't reveal what I shouldn't.

"It was pretty simple, just a painting of the two of us. You were sitting on a heavy armchair with a high back, you had a green dress on. What else... Your hair was up. Like this..."

I move closer to gather her hair in a quick bun, holding it with one hand and messing a few curls by her brow. My hand still at the back of her head, I lean away as much as possible to judge the general effect. It looks more or less like in my memory. Except...

Seeing her from that close, I realise how much the painting was lacking. It didn't show the way a light blush can bring out a few faded sunspots by her nose. Nor the tempting glint in her eyes, how her lips look slightly parted...

I drop my hand and fall back, a little out of breath.

"So yeah. Up like that," I manage to say.

"Yes. I see..." she answers, also looking a little distraught for some reason. "And, ah... What about you?"

It takes me a second too long to refocus.

"I was standing up. By your armchair. And I was looking at you, my face mostly hidden by my hair."

"How can you be sure it was you, then?"

I raise my sleeve a little, enough to give her a peak of the lines on my wrist.

"I saw those, and they were mine, that's certain. But also, my hair was still short, though less than now," I say, tugging on an uneven strand.

"I see... Was there anything else?" she asks, her eyes following my movement.

I look down at her hand, wondering an instant what her skin would feel like against mine, but blink to disperse the thought.

"No," I lie. "Nothing else."

***

After dinner that day, Ann follows me to the kitchen as I'm carrying back empty plates. I don't try to hide my smile because I know what's coming.

Since we were asked to leave Ann's room by Mrs Allander—after we got so absorbed by our brainstorming that we nearly missed lunch—Ann kept coming to me with new theories, which got crazier by the hour.

While a neighbour was here for tea, Ann suddenly gestured at me to follow her to the piano as if to show me some music sheets. Her back turned to the room, she whispered very seriously:

"Could you have ingested a potion?"

"A... potion?" I repeated, not sure I heard right. "Did you make me come here to ask if I drank a potion that threw me back in time?"

She nodded eagerly, and I was almost disappointed to have to ruin her theory.

"Once upon a time, I wasn't so careful as to what I was drinking, but that was a while ago. So no, I did not ingest a magical potion."

She scowled and went back to her seat. The guest had to repeat their question four times before Ann remembered their presence.

Later, a large shadow loomed over me as I was crouching in the garden with Alice. With the help of a book from the library, we were trying to understand which wild herbs were edible and which would kill us. In other words, a normal late afternoon activity to do with a child.

Alice shrieked at this sudden appearance, and I jumped to my feet, only relaxing when I recognised Ann. She dragged me away from her sister before asking,

"Did you meet a stranger who promised you something special? A gift or a favour, perhaps?"

"Even if I did, I wouldn't have asked to be sent to 19th century England, however how interesting," I answered dryly.

"What if you did not have a choice? Did you happen to hear someone whisper something behind you? Whilst you were looking at the painting?"

I laid a hand on her shoulder, her eyes following my gesture and my hand dropping immediately.

"I didn't accept anything from anyone or talked to anyone suspicious, because stranger danger," I said to reassure her.

Ann answered with the confused expression she always wears when my speech makes no sense to her, the one that amuses me endlessly.

"Better luck next time?"

She stood there a little longer while I went back to Alice, who was busy stabbing the ground with her spade for a reason only known to her. I didn't turn around when the shadow disappeared.

And now, I can feel Ann close behind me, almost pushing me forward in her impatience.

"Let me put that down first..." I say, amused.

I set the plates by the other dirty dishes before turning to face her.

"Right. What's the theory now?"

"I am holding you back here," she says. "I am the reason you are here, away from your friends and family."

Oh.

"I am, aren't I..." she whispers to herself with a defeated look on her face.

"Well... It's possible?" I say with a shrug, a little uncomfortable to see her distraught. "But—"

"No," she interrupts. "I think I know what to do."

Arms crossed, I lean against the counter, waiting.

"We need the painting," she says, surprising me.

"Why?"

"Because if I am the reason you are here, the painting is the medium that brought you here."

"Which means that..." I think aloud. "If we had the painting... If I touched it... I could probably go back?"

Ann nods at that, her expression conflicted for some reason. I bite the inside of my cheek as I think. There are many unknown parameters that could make this fail, but again, what do I have to lose?

"I guess it's worth a try," I say, a spark of hope flashing inside me, mixed with something else. "Except I don't know any painter. Well, apart from all those who will become famous later on, but we're a few decades too early for my favourites..."

"I do," Ann answers curtly.

She exits the room without another word, leaving me confused and wondering.

Chapter
Twenty-One

Suddenly, the neighbours seem to develop a deep affection for the Allander family because they're invited everywhere. For tea, for lunches, for walks and visits… It keeps the two oldest sisters and their mother busy. In fact, I barely see any of them for a few days, Mrs Allander having decided that I should stay home "to look after Alice". Which is an indirect way to ensure that I don't create disasters. But it's more than fine by me.

I spend most of my days with Alice and Janet, helping or playing around the house. When the weather allows it, we explore the paths nearby while waiting for the others to come home, exhausted by their social obligations.

As for the evenings, Mrs Allander has for rule that when possible, they should be reserved for the family—and me—declining all invitations. Mostly, we sit in the parlour, reading aloud or to ourselves, chatting, them teaching me card games…

I start laughing and smiling more easily, maybe because sharing my burden with Ann makes it more bearable. Definitively not because I grew fond of all of them, which would be irresponsible. I do have to go back, eventually.

Yet those evenings we spend all together might be what I look forward to the most each morning.

Okay, no. That's a lie.

My favourite moment of the day comes after we all leave for bed. I follow Ann to the room, always letting her lead the way, and we take turns changing behind the bedsheet she hung between the shelf above her desk and her dressing door. This new addition saddens me a little because making her blush remains my greatest joy.

Usually, by the time I'm done, she's already under her sheets, a book I know she won't read resting on her stomach. I join her, laying on my side, one arm under my head, and she settles more comfortably, her eyes always on me.

Then her questions start. Once she moved on from her initial disbelief, her curiosity and wonder took over. I love seeing the yearning in her eyes when I describe the countries I visited, the planes, the cities, the people. Her shock and awe when I recount my university years, my courses as well as my lost moments. Her surprise when I tell her about jobs I had, how I finally found a position I loved in a record shop after a long string of failed career choices.

Explaining what this job is turns out to be more complicated than expected, but it leads to music and art and books. That covers a few nights thanks to Ann's endless curiosity. I'm only too happy to oblige, only regretting that she can't experience it first-hand.

But I keep that to myself.

Rapidly, it becomes more of a conversation than a monologue. Ann talks about her family and her father, the struggles they had fitting in with the neighbouring society after his death and the financial worries that ensued. She speaks of her wishes for her sisters, for them to know the life they deserve and of her fear that she doesn't know how to make it happen.

"Nothing is set in stone," I tell her, patting her hand. "Look at me being here. There's always room for the unexpected."

She nods hesitantly at that, her eyes lowered.

And soon, my nights with her don't seem long enough, sleep always claiming us too quickly. There's so much more I want to know and tell her. I want to keep every precious confidence she shares with me in a special corner of my memory, carrying them with me always. Long gone is the coldness she affected towards me at the beginning. She's in turn funny, wicked-smart, cynical and sarcastic, quiet and thoughtful. She's made of infinite layers that leave me so much to discover.

But when I realise craving her presence during the day and being annoyed when yet another boring neighbour steals her away, I decide that a bit of distance maybe isn't all bad...

I still complain for the sake of it.

"Perhaps you should come today if you dislike us being away so?" Ann says, amused. "We are expected for an enlightening game of twist at the Cuttinghams'."

I groan and hide my face against Alice's shoulder.

"Worst combination of words ever."

"What an excellent idea, Ann. Let us all go," Mrs Allander decides suddenly, taking us all by surprise.

She puts down her fork by her empty plate and clears away a few breakfast crumbs from her skirt before looking at me and saying,

"It would be good for Lady Cuttingham to see our family all to-gether."

I'm about to protest that as I'm not actually part of the family, I should be exempted. But Alice looks at me, and from her eager expression, I can tell that for some reason she does want to go. So well. Who am I to ruin her fun?

"I guess..." I surrender finally, looking at Alma to see what she thinks of it all.

Her expression is unreadable, as every time the Cuttinghams are mentioned. She smiles back, a little mechanically maybe, before finishing her tea.

***

Weather allowing it, we decide to walk to our doom. See also: The Cuttinghams'.

Instead of joining Ann as my instinct urges me to, I step beside Alma, who seems surprised by it. I catch a glance of Ann's confused expression before she turns to her mother, Alice running in front of them.

"An unexpected pleasure," Alma says with a quiet smile.

"Is sarcasm a pre-requisite in your family?"

"Only an heirloom passed down from generation to generation."

As we both chuckle, I'm relieved to see her expression lose the uncomfortable stillness it had since breakfast.

"Are you ok?" I ask, lowering my voice a little.

"Of course. Why wouldn't I be?"

"Because we're off to try and pawn you to that miserable little man?"

"It is a creative way to describe the situation."

"Are you really going to marry him?"

"Well, he has not made his intentions clear as of yet, but if he does... When he does..."

She drifts off then, lost in thoughts I wish I could rip from her mind and stomp under my uncomfortable flat shoes.

"Would it be so terrible to not be married?"

"It has never been an option," she says in a definitive tone. "It is not only me I must think of, but of my sisters and mother as well. Even when Ann marries, it is possible that it will not be enough to ensure a comfortable life for Mother and Alice until she is of age."

Several disagreeable feelings swirl in my chest at that. I do my best to ignore them, instead focusing on a possible alternative.

"Maybe you should go travelling?" I try, remembering pages and pages of similar plot from books. "That's what people do here, right? You travel and you go to balls or whatever and you meet someone, you fall in love and *voilà*!"

Her smile turns sad.

"We do not have the means for me to travel."

"But Ann—"

"Ann's situation was different. She was asked to help an elderly neighbour join her in-laws' residence in the North. From what I understand, although she was given liberties, she was seen as no more than the help."

"I'm sorry, what?"

Alma shrugs, a gesture she absolutely got from me. I make a mental note to ask more about it to Ann later tonight. This reminder of our night chats rouses a thrill in me, but I snuff it, focusing on Alma once more.

"Let us hope this visit will be nothing more than a social occasion," she sighs.

***

Eager not to repeat past mistakes, I opt for complete silence, hoping my determination will be a good enough barrier for my big mouth. The good thing is that it makes Lady Cuttingham seem to be able to stand me. Especially as I let her beat me flatly at the incomprehensible card game. The not-so-good thing is that her silly nephew takes it as an opportunity to waste Alma's time by talking to her incessantly.

After a couple of hours of that, he asks her to "take a tour of the garden if only her kind sister would be kind enough to kindly chaperone". I roll my eyes before noticing that Mrs Allander and Ann froze in their seats. Alma's face lost all colours. Even Alice seems upset.

When Ann gets up, I follow suit, explaining that I need fresh air after the excitement of such a riveting game. Alma and Bland Man are leading, a little distance between us.

"What's going on?" I whisper to Ann.

"It seems M. Cuttingham is going to propose," she says, trying her best to hide the sadness in her voice.

I look at the scene unfolding in front of my eyes, disgusted. Alma has her back turned to us, but the tension in her frame appears clearly when Cuttingham kneels in front of her.

"We can't let that happen!" I protest to Ann.

"I am afraid there is no other choice."

I stare at her blankly.

"If you're not going to do anything, I will."

But as I begin to rush forward, Ann grabs my hand, squeezing it, her nails digging into my skin.

That's when I notice the tears in her eyes and the bitter turn of her mouth.

"Oh, Ann..."

So I don't do anything. I stay, moving closer to her, unable to look at Alma's life being destroyed.

But then.

We hear a voice calling from the terrace. Alice is waving wildly at us, pointing at the room behind her. Though she isn't close enough so that we can hear her exact words, the message is clear: we're expected inside immediately.

Alma also seems to have noticed the signal because she comes rushing back to us, leaving a very confused Cuttingham kneeling on the ground.

"He did not have time to finish his proposal," she whispers to her sister as we start towards the terrace. "Forgive me, Ann, but I cannot do it. I cannot accept this man. Please do not leave me alone with him again today."

When she moves to grab her sister's arm, Ann seems to remember she's still holding the hand by which she's dragging me forward. She drops it as if my skin burned hers.

The parlour is busy with newcomers when we return, two men in their mid-twenties, well-dressed, a smile on their face. They stand at ease, one of them leading Mrs Allander back to her seat, while the second is engaged in a polite chat with Lady Cuttingham.

All eyes converge to us when we enter the room however, conversation stopping. Alma and I exchange a curious look, but it's Ann who speaks first.

"Jeremiah!" she exclaims, startled, before stammering. "M. Twain, what a surprise it is! To see you!"

"So it seems," the man leading Mrs Allander answers warmly.

"*Jeremiah*?" I whisper to Alma, who looks as lost as I am.

The man—M. Twain—joins Ann to drop a kiss on her extended hand. I clench my teeth.

"My apologies for not warning you of my coming, but Benedict here said he received a letter from you asking for a visit," Twain explains. "I simply could not resist the temptation of meeting with you again so soon. And when your maid informed us you were visiting Lady Cuttingham, we thought appropriate to come and introduce ourselves, as we will be neighbours for the summer."

His attention is wholly focused on Ann, who can't seem to regain her composure. Someone clears their throat behind Twain, and he turns to Alma and bows before looking at Ann.

"Ah yes, of course," she says rapidly. "Please allow me to introduce my sister, Miss Alma Allander."

Then they move on to me. It's possible I forget to answer his polite bow.

"And, ah. Miss Max Jones, a guest of ours."

I nod briefly, even more annoyed when he doesn't seem discouraged by my rebuttal.

"Miss Jones comes from the colonies," Lady Cuttingham chips in, the word making me scowl dangerously.

"Is that so! You must have many riveting stories to tell then," the second man says, approaching.

I immediately take a liking to him, mostly because he doesn't make Ann stutter or try to kiss any limb.

"So pleased to meet you," I say in a sweet voice, grabbing his hand to shake it vigorously.

Though visibly confused, he goes along with it, smiling.

"Miss Jones seems as fascinating as you described, dear Miss Allander," he says to Ann with a bow.

"M. Kenilworth, please meet my sister," Ann replies, her hand touching Alma's elbow briefly. "And Alice, my youngest sister..."

Alice waves from the couch.

"And my mother, whom you seem to have already met."

"Indeed. What a lovely family you have, dear Ann!"

I scoff. What is it with those guys and their familiarity?

"Please sit," Lady Cuttingham says, reminding me of her presence.

Twain gives his arm to Ann as if she wasn't able to make it to the couch on her own. Kenilworth repeats the gesture to Alma, who smiles kindly at him. I snort when I realise that Cuttingham has just returned, watching Alma sit next to Kenilworth like an abandoned puppy. Feeling a little pity for the sad man, I extend my arm to him, but he only jumps back and disappears into the garden.

With a shrug, I move to sit by Alice, directly facing Ann and Twain, who are already lost in a conversation of their own. I try to remember my promise to myself to stay quiet, to not make a mess. But Ann laughs at something the man says and I—

"So. How did you all meet?" I ask too loudly.

Silence falls until Ann and the two men start to answer at once, then laugh. She touches Twain's arm not briefly enough.

"Well?" I insist, a little impatiently.

They exchange a look and a smile, and Ann takes the lead.

"We met at a private soirée when I was in the North. None of us knew anyone, and we struck a conversation about the... number of candles, if I remember well?" she says, looking at Twain.

"Indeed," he confirms. "And to express the interminable length of that evening, by the time we retired, we had counted all of them. 258 candles, to be exact."

"Even the ones in the garden," Kenilworth adds, making the three of them laugh again.

"Ha ha," I say before pointing at the two men in turn. "And who are you two, exactly?"

"Max!" I hear Mrs Allander protest in a low voice.

"My apologies. Who are you two exactly, *kind gentlemen*?" I say with my sharpest smile.

Alice chuckles and settles more comfortably at my side, looking pleased at the turn of events. That's when I understand why she was so eager to come.

Chaos.

"I believe it is quite a long story for a first visit," Twain says with a small bow to Lady Cuttingham, who seems pleased to be remembered. "But perhaps if Mrs Allander and the Misses Allander would grant us the pleasure of visiting them at home, we could discuss this more?"

"But of course, Sir," Mrs Allander answers gracefully, ignoring my seething. "We would be honoured to receive you."

"It is decided then," Kenilworth says brightly, already standing up. "My apologies to all of you ladies for the shortness of our visit, but we are expected in town tonight."

"Indeed," Twain confirms with a prolonged look to Ann. "We shall return in no longer than a few days and I hope we will have the pleasure of meeting again then."

"Can't wait," I mutter under my breath.

Ensues the bows and empty compliments to all. Kenilworth shakes my hand gladly and Twain follows suit, though he seems a little more reluctant.

Once they're gone, Ann struggles to pay attention to Lady Cuttingham's prattle. She's only dragged away from her thoughts when Alma comes to sit by her, engaging in a conversation in a low voice.

A look from Mrs Allander is enough to make me feel a little ashamed of my annoyance and confused as to where it comes from. After all, I don't know the two men at all, and if Ann likes them, they must be good people.

But then, I remember Twain's lips on Ann's hand and her flustered expression at seeing him. The same feelings return, amplified by the sisterly conversation I'm kept from.

Chapter Twenty-Two

On our way back, I stay a few steps behind, just close enough to hear but not particularly eager to join Ann's interrogation, led by Alma and their mother. The former's enthusiastic questions grate me more than they should. I try and fail to ignore this ridiculous feeling.

Ann retells the story of her first meeting with the two men, the few outings that followed, and the promise they made of seeing each other again. Which brings us to now.

When Alma asks her sister why she sent a letter to Kenilworth, she then ponders with a grin if Ann really did not expect Twain to join, even just a little. Ann has the audacity to blush. I slow down to add more distance between us.

By the time I get to the house, some time after the Allanders, I find them in the parlour, still engaged with the same subject. So I immediately step back, grab my boots from the future—which Janet hid in the entrance cupboard—and make for the backdoor.

"Max?"

I freeze momentarily at Ann's voice before resuming lacing my boots.

"Could we talk for a moment?" she continues.

I feel a sudden burst of irritation, not quite sure why.

"Later. I'm going to work in the garden."

"I see..."

Ann looks at me a little longer while I struggle to lace my boots for some reason, then she returns to the parlour. I wrench the door open, stomping towards the growing patch of herbs and vegetables with an impression of *déjà vu*, and get to work, barely noticing what I'm doing, my mind drowning in questions.

Why am I that annoyed? Those two men could mean good things for the family. They look rich but decent. Twain is clearly interested in Ann. She would be able to provide for her mother and sisters. And it could open up their social circle, allowing Alma to meet a better match, maybe.

But. What would it mean for me? If Ann gets busy with wedding stuff, how are we supposed to solve my mystery? How am I supposed to go back?

There's something else tugging at a corner of my mind, another disturbance I can't name... But I dismiss it, holding on to the slight relief I feel at having found the probable reason for my reaction.

It doesn't, however, give me any guidance as to what to do now.

Relentlessly, evening comes and Alma calls me to dinner. Unable to delay any longer, I gather my muddy tools and head back, ignoring all the concerned looks at my sudden silence. During dinner, I push the food around my plate and count the minutes until we're free to leave the table.

As soon as Janet brings dessert, I stand up too abruptly and gather a few plates, heading for the kitchen. I look around helplessly, debating whether to return to the table or to disappear upstairs. My brain feels on fire. I don't know what to do.

So I roll up my sleeves, tugging them above my elbows, and plunge my arms into the bucket of water to clean plates, pans and knives, whatever I can find to distract myself.

"Miss?" Janet says hesitantly as she enters the kitchen.

"Just call me Max. I've asked you to before."

"Ma—Max," she tries before changing her mind. "Miss Max. Mrs Allander is wondering if you will join them for tonight's reading in the parlour?"

"No. I'm busy," I say, scrubbing harder, dirty water splashing on my dress, dark stains spreading on the soft fabric.

Janet's confusion is almost tangible, but gratefully, she doesn't insist and only leaves the room.

As my thoughts from earlier return to swirl in my mind, unreachable, I start a deep clean of the table and the stove, narrowly avoiding burning my hand. It feels like hours go by as I work, sweat rolling down my cheeks, my hair flying wildly, my arms aching. It's only when I take a second to sit that I realise Janet is back, apparently at a loss as to what to do now that I've taken control of her kitchen.

Sheepishly, I look around, then at her.

"Sorry. I got carried away."

She smiles kindly at me, if a little worried.

"Far from me to complain. It isn't every day I have a moment to rest after the family's dinner," she says as she comes to sit in front of me at the table.

I stretch, relishing the soreness of my arms, but don't offer an answer.

"Mrs Allander informed me that you did not eat enough during dinner," Janet tries again. "She said you might be hungry by now?"

"I'm fine."

Of course, my stomach decides to betray me with a loud gurgle. I can't help but smile when Janet laughs, but then she puts her apron back on and I realise I've just added to her workload. So I ask:

"Did you? Eat, I mean."

"Oh, of course not! I never do before I have finished my chores."

I glance at the half-full pots on the newly cleaned stove and stand up, pushing Janet back towards the bench.

"Let's eat together then. And let me serve you for once. You deserve it."

I can see that Janet wants to intervene when she sees me struggling with the stove. But she sits patiently, only getting up to set up the table for the two of us.

Sitting in the warm kitchen, a plate filled with homely food in front of me, and engaging in an easy conversation feels good. Janet laughs at my jokes and almost makes me spit out my food when she tells me a daring one in her quiet voice. We talk about her home, her family, her childhood. Too soon our plates are empty, but we keep on chatting while she shows me how to correctly prepare tea.

It's only when the clock strikes ten that Janet seems to remember where she is. She rushes to the parlour in a panic despite my telling her not to worry, that I'll explain to Mrs Allander that I distracted her. She comes back a little calmer, saying that Miss Ann is still awake and about to retire to her room, that all is well.

Sure.

All is well.

***

"I trust you had a fascinating conversation with Janet," Ann says, a little coldly maybe.

I close the bedroom door, then step behind the spread bedsheet to change.

"It was lovely, yeah."

"When I asked if we could talk, I expected us to do so before morning comes."

"I'm sure that whatever you want to say can wait."

"I would rather it did not."

Not bothering to answer, I shuffle out of my clothes, cold feet meeting the floor. Ann pushes past the bedsheet, her eyes a thunder.

"Hey!" I protest, quickly pulling on the nightdress before remembering Ann is normally the prude one.

"Are we again to be on unfriendly terms?" she asks, her voice tense.

"You tell me, you're the one that usually decides of that."

"Yet it seems I did you wrong somehow, considering how openly you avoid me."

"Not everything is about you," I shoot back too quickly.

"Isn't it this time?"

I roll my eyes dismissively, as if she was wrong.

"Is it related to M. Twain and M. Kenilworth?" she guesses.

"I don't care about them."

"Yet hearing their names seems to anger you. Why is that?"

"No."

"Are you worried they will distract me from our mystery? That I will cease to help you find a way back?"

I grumble a little, annoyed to be read so easily.

"It seems my guess was correct," she congratulates herself, but I cut short to it.

"The faster we sort this out, the faster I can go back to my own time. The faster you're free to do what you want with Stain or whatever his name is."

I move past her towards the bed, trying to ignore her footsteps following me.

"You are perfectly aware what his name is. We both know by now that your memory is selective when you choose it to be. And are you implying that I am eager to solve your situation to be, as you say, free?"

"I'm not implying anything. We agreed I wouldn't involve myself in this whole marriage business and I won't. So, can I please go to sleep now?"

I'm half-expecting her to deny having thoughts of marriage, but she doesn't. I roll on my side, my back to her. Without another word, she blows the candle and settles next to me, immobile for a long time.

"M. Kenilworth is a painter," she says, her voice quiet in the dark.

"Good for him."

Silence returns between us until a realization drops heavily on me.

"Oh."

"Yes," she says. "Oh."

I can almost hear the smile in her voice. Rolling to the left, I meet her gaze briefly as she lies on her side, facing me.

We are so close.

"You asked him to come paint our portrait."

"Indeed."

"And he accepted? Without weird questions?"

"Well, he is here, isn't he? If he has questions, he did not share them with me yet. I believe he returned to London partly to purchase what he needs now that he has seen us both."

"Right."

I shuffle awkwardly for a moment, wincing.

"I, hm. I guess I'm sorry I was rude earlier."

I dare to look at her then, the white of her eyes clear in the dark, the amused curve of her lips as she smiles. Her hair tumbling down from her shoulder to the pillow, fanning across it. She slides one hand under her cheek, and I find myself wanting to move closer.

Which is when a second realization comes crashing down on me.

I am angry at Twain.

Because I'm jealous.

Because I like Ann very much.

In a "Oh no, she's beautiful and awesome and I want to put my face on hers" way.

That's bad. That's very, very bad.

And still, I can't stop gazing at her as she studies me with a curious look.

"Is everything well, Max? You seem flushed."

"Yup, all good. Perfectly good."

"Well, I am glad to hear so," she says, a slight frown still on. "I do hope it means you will act more friendly towards our two gentlemen friends when they come for a visit?"

The sudden surprise and, if I'm honest, excitement I felt at understanding what that nagging thing was, evaporates.

"Do you want Twain to come?"

"He is a kind friend and an excellent conversationalist."

"That's one shining review."

"If you had made an effort to talk with him, I am sure you would understand our friendship."

I mumble an answer, myself unsure of what I'm trying to say. Still, I can't help feeling a little relieved at the word "friendship".

Some time passes and I'm beginning to think Ann fell asleep when she speaks again.

"Do you have dear friends in your time?"

Her question takes me by surprise. Though the word "yes" readily pops into my mind, it's not what leaves my lips.

"I have... people I know."

"Friends and acquaintances are two different words."

"I meet a lot of people every day," I say, hating that I sound like I'm trying to justify myself. "You know, through my work and the places I lived in..."

"But do you rely on any of those people? Are you close?"

"Things can change quickly, so well," I say, lowering my eyes to look anywhere but at her.

"It seems you are trying to elude my question."

I don't contradict her, instead attacking the skin on my finger, moving on to the next one when it starts bleeding a little. Ann swats gently at my hand, bringing my attention back to her.

"Some time ago, you mentioned dear friends you lived with. Are they not part of your life anymore?"

"As I said, things change. They grew up, I didn't. We didn't want the same things anymore. So we went our separate ways."

"And what is it you want?"

Images of my relationships of all nature flood my mind. Memories of failures, anger and resentment. A bitter twist settles on my lips.

"I just want someone that understands me. That doesn't judge me. That doesn't make me feel like I need to change."

"A person who does cannot be called a friend," Ann says sharply.

"That's how most of the relationships in my life have been, though. Not that I'm not to blame. I don't think I'm always a good person and I know I've hurt people—"

My voice cracks when Ann lays her warm hand on my cheek, her resolute eyes meeting mine.

"Do you mean your family?"

I lean away at that, immediately closing off. Ann studies me for a moment before continuing in a soft voice, as if not to frighten me.

"You never mentioned your family, except in the story you told my mother and sisters. Though I doubt much of that is the truth."

"Because there isn't much to mention."

I hate hearing the pain and the fear seeping through my voice. It shouldn't affect me that much, it has no right to. I wrench my brain to think of a way to escape this unwanted conversation, but come up empty. Hurtful words and images hurl through my memories. I close my eyes tightly and turn my head away from Ann, hoping to dismiss this moment of weakness back to the hell where it came from.

But of course, Ann doesn't let go. She moves a little closer, brushing my hair away from my face in a slow motion. I let her for a moment before finding my voice again.

"I don't want to talk about that. There's nothing to say."

Ann doesn't answer, her hand still smoothing my hair at a calming rhythm.

We lay there in silence for a long time until, inexplicably, despite the misery those memories bring me, I find myself retelling the story of how I lost the people that were meant to be there for me, keeping quiet what needs to be. How accepting myself became what tore us apart. How I should have tried harder to find a balance between who I was and who they wanted me to be. Words bring back to life those moments I buried deep, anguish coursing through my body, fast as poison. When the last of it has left my lips, I can't bring myself to look at Ann, to find pity in her eyes. Her hand stills on my hair when she speaks, softly, sincerely.

"It is easy to blame oneself. It is more difficult to accept that not all fault rests on you."

When she takes back her hand, I want to follow, wondering if the rest of her is as warm as I'm cold. The impulse is broken when she lies on her back, eyes to the ceiling.

"Was there ever someone truly special to you?" she asks, her tone neutral.

I can't seem to be able to wrench my gaze from her, the soft glow of the moon lighting up her profile perfectly, as if we were in a freaking romance novel.

"No one that ever stayed."

All the guilt I feel towards Kate disappears when Ann turns her head towards me, a glorious smile on her lips.

"You deserve someone who stays," she says before closing her eyes, leaving me to turn her words in my head for hours.

Chapter Twenty-Three

The morning brings fresh excitement.

First, a letter from Twain. He writes that he's so very sorry, but they won't be able to come back before the ball in two weeks, the mention of which leaves us all confused. Then a second letter, an invitation to a ball at Squareshaw Park, the house both men are renting near Merton, which, according to Alma, isn't very far.

As Ann keeps reading, it becomes clear that it's also an invitation to stay for a few days, addressed to all of us, Alice included. She is about to burst with joy at the news, already excited about what it entails. Sadly for her, Mrs Allander cuts short to it when she announces that Alice and herself will stay home, only meeting us on the day of the ball.

I wince at Alice's clear disappointment and think for a minute to propose to stay with her. But then, I realise it would mean that Ann and Twain—and the other two, of course—would be left alone and I'm not too keen on the idea. So I keep my mouth shut, even when Alice looks at me pleadingly, then storms out when I don't volunteer to help. I sigh, promising to redeem myself somehow.

Mrs Allander informs me that in her absence, I'm to be some sort of chaperone, which confuses me at first, until she explains that it means I'm off the marriage market. Which is super fine by me. Ann and Alma are already discussing what we will need, what to bring, how to get there. I sit patiently, waiting for them to include me in the conversation.

"A green dress would be wonderful," Ann says with a quick glance at me. "I should like one that is elegant enough for such a ball, yet easy to wear for another occasion. Perhaps for an outing or if M. Kenilworth happens to be in a creative mind?"

The meaning of her words hits me then, and I nod fervently.

"Yeah, green will fit you for sure. I'll find the... appropriate dress as well."

The complicit look we exchange seems to confuse Alma, but Mrs Allander interrupts our private scheming.

"I do not think we have the means for new dresses, my dears. I am sorry. We will have to make do with what we have."

"I can arrange another one of mine for Max," Alma says. "I believe it would do just fine."

"And I am sure the occasion for new dresses will present itself soon," Ann adds, sensing my disappointment at our failed plan.

Ann and Alma fall back in their conversation. I glance at Mrs Allander, who seems lost in thought.

"Max, would you be kind enough to give us a moment?" she asks then.

I nod and exit the room, but curiosity gets the best of me. Quietly rushing through the corridors, I reach the other door, glad to see that Janet didn't close it completely earlier.

"I believe you both understand what this could mean," I hear Mrsl-lander say. "These two gentlemen are of means and Ann, dear, you seem to esteem them well enough?"

One of them—Ann probably—gets up and starts pacing slowly.

"Yes, Mother, I know them to be good and kind men."

"Do you believe them to be good matches for you and your sister?"

I can't say I'm surprised to hear that this is what Mrs Allander has in mind, but it stings nonetheless.

"I…"

What surprises me is to hear Ann hesitate. From the way she reacted seeing the two men and her insistence that I try to be friendly with them, I assumed she had the same idea.

"I know M. Twain enough to say with certainty that we would be a good match. However, I do not think I should decide for my sister if she could grow to love M. Kenilworth."

"Love is not essential," Alma says. "A good life companion is all I could hope for."

"But I want love for you. And I do not think M. Kenilworth could be the person to give you that."

"I believe it is for me to decide. It appears I cannot force myself to marry someone such as M. Cuttingham. But if M. Kenilworth reveals himself to be as decent and kind as you describe him to be, then it is more than I require."

"Alma…"

"I dislike the idea of rushing you before you are well and truly ready," Mrs Allander says to close the matter, "but I do hope this stay at Squareshaw Park brings you the answers you need."

I move away from the door, stunned by the clear-headed calculations they have to resort to. They're aiming for a life of tolerating their partner, of being married to someone who is basically a stranger. For comfort and money. They have to offer themselves to the highest bidder to be able to provide for their family, because they're seen as nothing but women. I'm not sure I would ever be able to decide of the rest of my life with such rationality. And it drives me insane that I can't do anything about their situation because I, myself, have to comply to my role of woman. I'm displaced and lost, sure, but it doesn't change the fact that my hands are tied here. All I can do is watch events unfold. Regardless of whatever feelings I seem to have caught.

But maybe... Maybe I could at least ensure that they are good for each other, that if they do marry, they don't do it blindly. I could help them to get to know each other better, with subtlety and discretion. Kenilworth and Alma, and Twain and... Ann.

What could go wrong?

Chapter
Twenty-Four

As I step out of the carriage, I freeze and turn to Ann, mouth agape.

"We're staying *here*?"

She glances at me before nodding gratefully at the man taking care of our luggage.

"Why, of course. What did you expect?"

"Not this!" I exclaim, gesturing wildly at the building.

A large and immaculate mansion—which I could accurately describe as a palace—looms over us. Its front is covered by three rows of windows and a large dark door through which a stream of people appears, all dressed in elegant livery. They stop at ease at the bottom of the stairs as Twain and Kenilworth come strutting down to meet us.

"Welcome, all!" Kenilworth greets us.

Dumbfounded as I am, I forget to react when he takes my hand to kiss it. But I clear my mind quickly enough before Twain has time to do the same. Instead, we shake hands, his smile neutral, me looking over his shoulder in awe.

"It seems Max is quite impressed by your house after residing in our humble abode for so long," Ann teases me, looking at Twain.

"What, no!" I protest. "But... Wow! I mean, I visited places like this, but it's usually crowded with tourists. I never imagined I would ever stay in one!"

"Tourists, you say?" Twain repeats. "I did not know such houses were opened to large groups. Is it a custom in the colonies?"

"Don't say colonies, it's repulsive," I chastise him. "And I meant—"

"She meant grand houses in London that she has seen during a visit there, before her time with us. You must be aware that renowned families like to display their wealth," Ann saves me, glancing at Twain with a smile.

"Only too well," he jokes back, gesturing at the castle behind him before offering his arm to Ann. "If you please? We have prepared tea in the south parlour. The view there is most exquisite."

They go up the stairs first and disappear inside the house. I glance at our luggage, but Kenilworth offers his left arm to me and his right one to Alma, and inside we go.

It's only because I don't want to seem even weirder that I don't gasp at each room we cross, amazed by everything I see. I've never been one for luxury, but this is fascinating.

What I'm seeing are not replicas or photos, but ancient—to me—paintings and furniture, instruments and sculptures. Every room is crowded with objects displaying an obvious wealth, as well as a certain lack of taste that doesn't fit the image I have of the two men.

"How long have you been living here?" I ask Kenilworth.

"Oh, we arrived but three days ago. This house is ours for the summer only and we longed to enjoy it as much as possible."

"You brought all your stuff just for the summer?" I reply, puzzled.

"'Stuff'?"

I gesture at everything surrounding us.

"Oh dear, no, those are not our belongings, but those of the family who own the house. Friends of the Twains. They will return from London in the autumn."

"It is quite a charming interior," Alma says neutrally.

I know her well enough now to be certain she finds it as terrible as I do.

"If I am to be honest with you, my tastes tend to be more... subtle," Kenilworth admits, eyeing a large baroque painting to our right. "I find my lodgings in the city to be a suitable reflection of that."

"Oh, really?" I say, seizing the opportunity to put my plan in motion. "That sounds so nice. I'm sure Alma would love to see your place sometimes!"

Alma blushes violently, but Kenilworth only smiles.

"I fear you would find it too humble to be interesting, especially as it is neglected by my spending so little time there, except to sometimes paint. Nonetheless, it would be my pleasure to welcome you and your family for a visit someday."

I pretend to study a horrifyingly graphic painting of Jesus to hide my victorious smile.

***

In the afternoon, it's decided that we should explore the garden. The size and variety of it is incredible, but my mind is focused on Alma and Kenilworth. They stand a little aside, discussing the plants and flowers or something. I'm too far away to hear. I notice some silences and awkward laughs, but it's only natural in every burgeoning relationship. I decide not to meddle for now, letting fate do its thing.

"Oh, this, I do not know. Max is our resident expert on the subject of gardening," I hear Ann say behind me.

Distracted, I glance at her before staring at Alma and Kenilworth some more.

"I think Max would know what this particular plant is," Ann says louder.

I sigh and turn around.

"Which one?" I ask, sparing a brief look at the ground. "Yeah, that's cucumber."

"How interesting," Twain says, vaguely prodding at the plant with his finger.

"So interesting, yes."

I turn to resume my observation, but Alma and Kenilworth are already walking back towards us, a little distance between them.

"Oh, come on," I mutter under my breath, earning a strange look from Ann.

***

The following day, we're all sitting aimlessly in one of the many rooms despite the beautiful weather outside, because that's apparently something people do here. Ann is on the couch in front of me, lost in a book. Twain and Kenilworth are writing ball-related letters and final invitations, and Alma is sketching by the window.

I slept badly the night before despite having my own bed for the first time in a while, but I don't have time to waste resting. Or to wonder why I couldn't sleep. While I pretend to be enraptured by the random book I picked, I'm actually studying everyone to sort out a plan. As I watch Alma glancing between her sketchbook and the outside, an idea comes to me. I join her and she looks up at me with a distracted smile.

"Well, isn't that a lovely drawing!" I exclaim too loudly, making Twain jump in surprise. "Those shapes and those... lines! M. Kenilworth, you're a painter, right? You should come see what Alma did! Seems like you share an interest in art."

"M. Kenilworth is busy, Max. Perhaps this can wait," Ann interjects, throwing me a sharp look that I ignore.

"Yes, and I would rather—" Alma says.

"But it's so nice! And with this light right now, wow!"

"If it is... 'wow', then I believe it is my duty as an artist to see for myself," Kenilworth says, amused.

"Truly, Sir, I do not believe—" Alma tries again.

Kenilworth stops behind Alma's seat, who looks down before handing him her sketchbook. He angles it under a sunray coming in, studying it carefully.

"This is indeed beautiful, Miss Allander, truly," he says. "I did not realise I was in the company of a fellow artist!"

"Quite a wonder," Twain adds more neutrally as he joins us, standing behind Kenilworth and looking over his shoulder.

"You must have studied arduously to reach this level of excellence!" Kenilworth continues. "May I ask who your masters were?"

"My sister never had a master. It is only the result of natural talent and hard work," Ann says, glaring at me for some reason. "She has also always been quite shy about her gift."

Ah. I glance at Alma, who's still staring at the floor.

"Why, you have no reason to be, Miss Allander," Kenilworth says. "A talent such as yours should be celebrated! If you would allow me, I would be honoured to share some of what I know with you."

Alma looks up at that, her eyes eager.

"Oh, Sir, what an opportunity it would be!"

"Benedict, do you think—" Twain starts.

He stops when he meets my menacing glare.

"What do you say we take an hour each evening to hone our skills?"

"With the highest pleasure, Sir!" Alma thanks him, her cheeks flushed.

As they begin to talk about techniques and colour theory, I sit back with the sentiment of a job well done. I try to catch Ann's eye to see if she shares my enthusiasm, but she seems to be engaged in a silent conversation with Twain. When he excuses himself for a moment, she follows.

Chapter Twenty-Five

By the next day, Kenilworth and Alma are spending every free minute together, their successful training session having already spread over several hours the evening before. I look at them from my spot in the grass, as he teaches her to compose a palette of oil colours that matches the lush shades of the garden.

I should have guessed it wouldn't take much for him to like Alma. The contrary seems impossible. And now that this is done, I can focus on...

Actually, I'm not that convinced yet that Alma and Kenilworth are properly interested in each other. They only talked about art and that does not a relationship make. I should definitively prod a little more.

Stretching lazily on the grass, I lose myself to my mental scheming, which is interrupted when Ann appears towering over me.

"Hey," I greet her with a relaxed smile. "Care to join me?"

But she looks away, her expression tense when she asks:

"Would you be kind enough to come with me for a moment?"

"No need to be so formal, you know? We've been sharing a bed for a while. We're past that."

She doesn't take the bait. So, with a sigh, I get up, dust my skirt free of grass and follow her back inside the house. She leads me to a room at the other end of the second floor from mine, which I'm successfully guessing to be hers.

"Ah, I have the same bedsheets. Fun," I say, settling comfortably as I would on our shared bed.

The familiar smell of candle wax, ink and fresh linen I came to associate with Ann surrounds me then. Delighted, I feel my eyelids getting heavier, but Ann slams the door shut. She rests her forehead against it and lets out an irritated hiss.

"Could you please be serious for just a moment?"

I immediately frown, confused as to what I could have done wrong this time.

"Whatever it is you are trying to achieve between my sister and M. Kenilworth—"

"It's that obvious, eh?" I beam, pleased that my efforts have been noticed.

"You must stop," Ann warns sharply.

My smile falls.

"You said you would not involve yourself in the question of our future husbands. Please continue to do so."

"I'm not doing anything bad though," I protest. "I just want to make sure she and him are a good match."

"I understand you mean well, but it cannot be."

"Why? She seems to like him, and he's nice, rich, good-looking, interesting. They're both artists."

"I may have asked you to stop, but do not misunderstand it as a request."

"I don't get you," I say, staring at her. "You say you want the best for Alma, but you were ready to let her marry Cuttingham. And now that there's a good-enough man whom she could actually like, you're putting yourself in her way?"

"I do want the best for her. And it isn't M. Kenilworth."

"But why?"

"It does not concern you."

"It kind of does though."

"It does not!" she explodes. "You are not part of our family. You have no right to meddle in our affairs! You are merely a guest."

And that... It hurts. A lot.

"Right," I say, getting up to leave. "Message received, loud and clear."

"Max, I didn't..."

I rush out of the room before I can hear more.

Chapter Twenty-Six

I spend the last two days before the big party, mostly on my own, only imposing my presence on the others when I can't avoid it. Seeing Alma and Kenilworth getting along so well now only deepens the wound, though I refuse to regret something I feel is right.

In an unspoken agreement, Ann doesn't try to speak to me, and I don't meet her eyes. When she enters a room, I promptly make an excuse to escape by the other door. I spend hours walking the grounds, hiding with a book I never read, waiting for the day when Mrs Allander comes and takes me back. But for what?

Ann is right. I'm nothing but a guest. One whose stay should have an expiry date. But the problem remains that my leaving rests on Ann and she made it clear that I was not a priority for now.

When I finally manage to catch Kenilworth alone to ask him when he could start working on the portrait, he admits he can't promise anything yet. He would need some quiet time after the ball for us to pose.

So that's just great.

On the afternoon of the ball, I ignore the maid's desperate plead for me to finish getting ready. Instead, I disappear down a path I found on my own, which leads to a shallow part of the woods surrounding the house. There, I sit on the ground, chin resting on my knees.

Though I already did it this morning, I count again how much time has passed since I first landed here. I come to the same conclusion. It has been a little more than eight weeks now. About five since Ann's arrival. Not for the first time, I wonder if my absence has been noted in 2022, if the people I know are worried. If anyone is missing me.

As tears flood my eyes, I suddenly wish I could simply blink and wake up in my own bed, in my small London flat, my flatmate's snores echoing through the wall, thinking this was all just a dream. I never belonged here, but being with the Allanders made me believe I did, even just for a moment, and it's wrong. The longing I feel for my own time is sudden, new and crushing. I want to go back. I have to go back.

When my name is called loudly from the house, I stand up and walk back, storing this new determination in my mind for after the ball.

**

By the time I come down, stupid feathers stuck in my hair and the too long dress Alma lent me hindering my steps, the party is already in full swing. I immediately spot Alma dancing, though not with Kenilworth, and Twain talking to an older man by the chimney.

Relieved not to fall on Ann immediately—and so not to have to disappear back to my room—I make my way through the crowd, looking for Mrs Allander and Alice. Who, of course, are with Ann. Wonderful.

Mrs Allander sits with her back to me, amicably discussing with a couple around her age. She acknowledges me with a smile when Alice shouts my name and bounces in my direction.

"Hey kiddo," I say, gathering her against me for a hug.

"Do not ever leave again, the house is an absolute bore without you there!" she whimpers, her voice muffled by the too large amount of frills I'm wearing.

I meet Ann's eyes above Alice's shoulder and my smile drops.

"Always exaggerating, eh," I say, quickly looking down at the girl.

Alice smiles wetly and grabs my hand.

"Let's catch up on lost time, shall we?" I say before leaning to whisper in her ear. "I know where they hid the desserts. What do you think? Should we attempt a stealth expedition?"

Alice stands straighter, a glint in her eye.

"Let's be brave in the face of danger!" she declares aloud, as I taught her.

I return her salute and we head towards the small reserve next to the kitchen, but not before I throw one last glance at Ann. Her expression seems wistful despite the casual smile on her face. Lowering my eyes, I do my best to push her to the back of my mind until later.

***

"Miss Jones, would you care to—"

"No," I say, stuffing my mouth with cake for good measure. "I'm busy."

Alice chuckles as the man moves away, whispering "Dear God" under his breath. Somehow, he isn't the first one I'm rejecting tonight. He'll get over it.

Our expedition was a success. Alice and I then retreated to a corner for the evening, one where we had a good view on the dancefloor while being away from what seemed to be the social centre of the room. It also happened to be close to the staff door, allowing me to snatch a fresh glass of fizzy alcohol every time an employee came back to the room. So many wins for me.

For some unknown reason, a few men came and decided to ask me to dance. After the fifth one, I ran out of creative excuses, instead opting for good old rudeness. I should have tried to make an effort as a guest of Twain's and Kenilworth's, but honestly, I couldn't find it in me to care.

Having spent most of the evening watching Ann dancing with Twain and smiling at him took a toll, my newfound jealousy eating at me like acid. Instead, I tried to focus on Kenilworth, who seemed to find every reason to refuse to dance, and on Alma, who grabbed every opportunity to be twirled on the dancefloor.

Partner after partner asked to be introduced to her and for a dance, but the last one had seemed different. First, because her neutral expression dropped after a few words from the unsmiling man, replaced by curiosity. Second, because they danced two more times until now. The change in her attitude was clear to all who knew her.

"What do you think?" I ask Alice, pointing at Alma dancing.

"Is it the same man again?" she says, squinting. "He seems old."

"Hey! He looks about my age."

"I said what I said," the little monster replies, devouring a spoonful of her cake.

"You're like 8, so of course everyone looks old to you."

"I am 12, soon to be 13!"

"Is that so? Congratulations are in order then," I say, spreading cream on her cheek.

She shrieks and tries to return the attack, but we're interrupted by Kenilworth.

"Miss Jones. Would you do me the honour of accepting my company for the next dance?" he says, looking more down than I have ever seen him so far.

And that's enough to make me curious. I turn to Alice, raising my eyebrows, and she glances at the man, then back at me and nods. We high-five discreetly between our skirts, and I get up to accept Kenilworth's arm.

"With pleasure, my dear sir."

A few whispers can be heard as we take place on the dancefloor. I realise it must be because one of the hosts had yet to dance and somehow, he chose me, the strange woman who probably has clotted cream on her face.

The dance is simple enough. I follow what people are doing around me and remember to hold the hem of my skirt not to trip on it. A few minutes go by without a word between us, Kenilworth still looking off.

"You're not feeling well?" I whisper as we meet for a hand wiggle thing.

My voice seems to drag him from whatever dark thoughts he was lost in.

"My apologies, Miss Jones. I am being a terrible partner."

"That's alright, I am not too keen on dancing either."

"Oh, it isn't that. I do love to dance... Unfortunately, the person I wish to dance with is otherwise engaged."

He glances over my shoulder before returning his attention to me with a sad smile. Turning my head, I spot Alma dancing with a new man, the stern looking one from earlier standing close. Ann is also there at the end of the row, dancing yet again with Twain, her gaze returning to her sister every few seconds.

"You just have to ask, you know?" I advise Kenilworth, conscious of my hypocrisy, but also of the difference in our situations.

"If only it were that simple," he sighs. "But let us forget about this for now. Pray tell me..."

When he changes the subject entirely, I comply. Though I can't help but notice that his attention strays often. When the dance finishes, I pat his arm.

"I'm sure it will work out."

"If only it were that simple..." he repeats, dispirited, before walking away.

***

On my way back to Alice, I'm chasing one of the men carrying a tray of precious alcohol when a hand lands on my arm.

"I don't want to dan—" I start to say, turning around.

I hold my breath when Ann moves a step closer as someone rudely makes their way behind her. She looks at me for a moment, her eyes conflicted.

"Are you enjoying the evening?" she asks politely.

"Oh yeah. Who doesn't like being trapped in a dress with frills and feathers?"

"I must agree it does not particularly suit you," she notes, looking up and down at me.

"Wow. Thanks for the vote of confidence. Again," I mutter, already walking away.

But Ann catches my wrist, bringing me to a halt and making me glare at her.

"Max, please," she whispers. "Those past few days... I have been wanting to apologise."

"You don't have to, you were right. I'm only a guest and I shouldn't involve myself in your lives. I've already managed to dance with Kenilworth without throwing him at your sister, noticed that?"

"It isn't... I wish I could explain..."

Though angry, seeing her lost expression pains me. I sigh and rub a hand on my face.

"Okay, you know what? I'll meet you in your room after the ball. I want to talk about me leaving. It's time."

"Max..."

"Later."

As I turn to go, I hear her voice following me despite the general clamour around us.

"I like you better in your own clothes."

I hurry away.

Chapter
Twenty-Seven

The rest of the evening goes in a blur of alcohol, cake and laughter with Alice until she is called to bed. Maybe a little staring at Ann as I try to figure out what I'm going to say to her. I feel a little too drunk to be able to hide from her what needs to be and not enough to have a dramatic conversation. So that promises to be interesting.

I manage to avoid the last moments of the ball by hiding on yet another balcony. It's only when the final guests depart that I emerge. The room is now quiet, except for the few employees cleaning. I ask if I can be of any help, but as expected, they panic and stutter that it would not be appropriate for me to do so. And as expected, I ignore them and gather plates and glasses to make it easier for them to carry away.

As the clock strikes one, I'm half hoping Ann will already be asleep. After all, it has been a long and exhausting evening. So much dancing. So much socialising. It's probably better to wait until tomorrow. I'm sure Ann would agree if I dared to ask her.

My decision taken, I make for the library to choose a book and clear my head a little. Not at all a distraction, of course, only a sudden longing for culture. I pick up the thickest book I can find and turn the chair away from the door before settling in it. Not that I am hiding. I just want to waste a little time before bed with this—I turn the book to look at the title—*Exposé on Modern Medicine*. I groan, but start to read anyway, wincing at every gruesome illustration. At least, it'll keep me busy for a while.

Flicking the pages distractedly, I'm surprised when the clock only chimes the half hour. With a sigh, I close the heavy book and slouch in the chair. That's when I hear footsteps outside the room and the sound of the door opening, then closing softly.

Undetermined noises follow. I want to look, but then, I would have to explain why I'm here at this hour, alone in the library. And my tipsy condition does not allow lies and dissimulation of facts. So I stay as still as possible, hoping for whoever it is to leave soon.

A thud resonates and a groan, as if... As if someone had been pushed against the shelves? Then, rustling and more groaning, and I press a hand against my mouth.

Oh no. Oh no no no.

The whimper that follows confirms what I stumbled upon. Though technically, *they* stumbled upon *me*. I hear some more kissing noises, followed by deep breathing—a man's—and then silence. Only for a few seconds.

"It is dangerous for us to be here like this."

I almost gasp when I recognise Twain's voice. Then blanch immediately at the thought that it could be Ann with him. If I had been to her room earlier...

"I know. But I could not stand being apart from you any longer."

I actually gasp at Kenilworth's voice, the noise stifled by my hand.

"Being forced to watch you from afar all evening—" he says quietly.

"I understand only too well, my love... But you know what is at stake. You know what it is all for."

I hear a kiss, then a soft sigh.

"Tell me again," Kenilworth whispers.

"It is for you, Benedict. Always for you..."

They leave only minutes later, bare feet shuffling on the carpet. But I stay hidden much longer, as if frozen, thoughts swirling in my head.

Chapter
Twenty-Eight

Eventually, I make my way up to the second floor, now glad that my room is so far away from Ann's. Once inside, I sit on the floor by the bed, face hidden against my folded arms.

Kenilworth and Twain are together. Looking back, I should have guessed. If I hadn't been so focused on Ann and on creating an impossible match, I would have. The super close friendship, the living and travelling together, Kenilworth's sadness earlier... He wasn't looking at Alma then, but at Twain.

But where does Ann fit in all of this? Does she know? Is she supposed to be the beard in the two men's relationship? I know—and despise—that homosexuality isn't legal nor accepted in this time. So what if Twain's interest in Ann is nothing but a tactic? Never love or affection? She deserves better and Twain should feel free to be with the man he clearly loves.

But again, what if she knows? What if she marries Twain on purpose to help him hide his relationship? What would it mean for her? I know Ann is kind and thoughtful, but it seems a little extreme, even for her.

Unless...

I look up, frowning. Money? Could it be the only reason? After all, Mrs Allander, Ann and Alma never hid that a possible match needed to be a wealthy one. Could Ann know and pretend not to for the money? Accept her future role because the reward is worth it? But what if she truly likes Twain? What if she is being played? Or what if she's... blackmailing him?

I shake my head at this last ridiculous one. Too many possibilities collide in my tired brain, and I can't seem to find an answer that makes sense. I can't ask Ann if she knows at the risk of outing the two men, which is an unbearable thought. But I also can't let her keep on believing her relationship with Twain is real because she will end up hurt.

Helpless, I bury my head back against my arms and let morning come.

***

At breakfast, I find it hard to look at anyone. Mrs Allander and Alice are supposed to leave in a couple of hours, and I plan to go with them. Though I haven't announced it yet.

I spent all night thinking the issue over and over and eventually concluded that the best I could do was to leave. Past experiences made it clear that only disaster results in me involving myself in that whole marriage nightmare. So keeping my distance is the logical thing to do. Ann is smart; whatever she decides will be the right choice for her.

Yet the same possibility keeps troubling my thoughts. What if she doesn't know and realises too late...

The fork I'm holding loosely falls onto the table with a clang, startling me from my worries. When Kenilworth meets my bewildered gaze with concern, I blush and look away. My traitorous gaze falls on Ann, who seems as tired as I feel.

"Thank you again, gentlemen, for your invitation," Mrs Allander says, visibly eager to dismiss the strange mood in the room. "And for your kindness towards my daughters."

"It has been a pleasure having them all with us this week," Kenilworth says agreeably.

"And I am certain our last few days together will be as charming," Twain adds with a brief look to Ann. "One of our neighbours yesterday asked us for the pleasure of a visit from the Misses Allander and Miss Jones—"

"Actually, I'm going to leave with Mrs Allander if that's okay," I chime in, staring straight at the wall above Kenilworth's head.

In the corner of my eye, I notice Ann sitting straighter and Alma looking confused, but it's Kenilworth who speaks.

"Are you feeling unwell, Miss Jones? Did you not enjoy yourself at the ball yesterday?"

"Oh no, it was all great. So great. But I feel, hm, tired? So it would be nice to be back at the Allanders'. Getting back to the old routine, you know?" I try to say as convincingly as possible.

Alice squeezes my hand with an excited smile.

"But of course," Twain replies with a concern that feels fake. "We are sorry to lose you, but I understand that social occasions can indeed be exhausting. And far from us to keep you from your young friend, who seems quite eager to get you back!"

Alice smiles blindingly at him. I glance at Ann, wincing at her lost expression.

"I'll go pack then," I say, standing up.

"I shall help," Ann adds immediately, leading the way out of the room.

I hesitate a second too long and get moving when the others start to look at me strangely.

***

We barely make it inside the room before Ann verbally slams into me.

"You confuse and aggravate me, Max!"

Looking away, I start gathering my spilled belongings and stuffing them in my wooden travel box.

"I'm sorry you think so."

"Why leave now, after the kindness M. Kenilworth and M. Twain showed us?"

"You don't need me here. I'm not the one they're after. And Alma's your sister, so it makes sense that she stays with you."

"But what if I want you here, too?"

Those. Those are the kind of words that made me wonder more than once last night if I completely misread Ann. If there isn't something more in the way she looks at me, in the way she speaks to me. I like to think I've always been quite good at noticing when someone was attracted to me. But with her, it's different and I don't know how to make sense of any of it.

The way she's looking at me now, her gaze holding mine... In my own time, with anyone, I would have taken it as an invitation to try my luck. If I misread the situation, I'd apologise. We would probably laugh about it and move on. But here, with her, I can't do that. Her family is my only anchor and Ann remains the key to my travelling back.

But. It's more than that and I know it.

I need to leave this house because I can't sleep at night when Ann isn't next to me. Because watching her with Twain, acting as if they were already married, makes me want to shove my head through a window. Because it doesn't matter if she knows his secret or not, or if she could share an ounce of what I feel for her. It won't ever come true because it can't. The society we are in wouldn't allow it, and eventually, our stories will diverge. And as I struggle not to reach for her, I realise it needs to be soon.

She breaks eye contact first, moving to the window, her back to me.

"M. Twain is a nice man," she says, her voice quiet.

"Nice. Yes. He's nice."

"And he has a good fortune. I would be provided for. I would be settled in a house of my own."

"Yes."

"My sisters' social status would be improved. And my mother would be proud and honoured to have such a gentleman in our family."

"Yes. He's a great option all around," I conclude curtly, eyes to the floor.

Ann turns around and sits on the windowsill, her voice hardening at my lack of reaction.

"You have done nothing but contradict me since the day we met. Yet now that I wish to discuss an important subject and desire your honest opinion, you keep it from me. Do you have to be so vexing?"

The pressure of the last week escapes the tight box where I hoped to keep it. That gut-wrenching feeling I felt watching Ann and Twain together emerges again, stronger. I clench my teeth to force the words back in.

What does she want me to say? If I could be honest, I would tell her to never marry him because the sight of them together is torture. That he doesn't really appreciate her for the smart, caring and astonishing person she is. But I do. And I want to be around her all the time because even just a second away feels like a waste.

"I'm sure you'll be happy together," is what I say instead.

After a moment, she leaves without another word, her arm brushing mine for the briefest of second before she's gone.

Chapter
Twenty-Nine

Because I—their chaperone—decided to leave, the sisters' visit at Squareshaw Park has to be cut short. Which means I have two days, three at most, to sort myself out before Ann and Alma are back.

So obviously, instead of dealing with anything useful, I play with Alice, hiding and jumping out on Janet when she least expects it. However, we're forced to stop when it causes her to drop the pot of soup meant for dinner and that we're left with dry bread and a few veggies.

When Mrs Allander and Alice are busy with the latter's lessons, I go for walks, but too quickly, my thoughts emerge back, more annoying than ever. So I hunt for distractions, arming myself with books from the library or helping Janet dust shelves and every flat surface in the house. I even polish cutlery, which is about the worst thing I ever forced myself to do.

But inevitably, every day ends. And every night, I find myself in our shared bed, left to imagine Ann beside me as we were for many evenings, sharing stories in low voices. And every night, unable to stand it, I retreat to the parlour, recreating my nest and sleeping fitfully to make sure I'm gone by the time anyone wakes up.

On the day of the sisters' return, I am in dire need of sleep. My mind is a mess and I'm too exhausted to even think about fixing it. Which might explain why, when I hear their carriage coming up the path, I run away to my spot at the far end of the park. I lay down to hide and, of course, I immediately fall asleep.

By the time I open my eyes, I'm not sure how much time has passed. Night has fallen, however, so I panic a little and rush back to the house. Janet's relieved shriek welcomes me.

"Mrs Allander! Miss Max has returned!"

I hear a door slam, and Ann comes barrelling down the corridor. She doesn't give me a chance to say "hi" before she grabs my shoulders with a little too much force.

"Where have you been?" she asks, frantic.

"First, ouch. Second, I was just in the park. I may have fallen asleep a little," I shrug before meeting her burning gaze and correcting myself. "A lot?"

"I—We were terrified! No one knew where you were. We thought you ran away!"

"Nowhere to go, remember," I say, shaking my shoulders to free myself from her grasp.

She jumps back as if burned and stomps upstairs without another word.

"Quite the temper, eh," I joke to Janet.

She only glares at me.

"Miss Ann was beside herself with worry when we couldn't find you. As were the other Misses and Mrs Allander. They are waiting in the parlour."

She disappears towards said room, leaving me alone to rub a hand on my face before following.

"Sorry!" I apologise as I enter the room, "I was tired, and I fell asleep and—"

At my interruption, Mrs Allander looks up from the letter she was apparently reading aloud.

"Oh, sorry," I repeat, raising both hands.

I go sit by Alice and wave at Alma, who nods back tightly before turning to her mother.

"Oh, no. What now?" I say, noticing the look and the letter.

"It is from M. Twain," Mrs Allander says.

That's enough for me to guess her next words.

"He is asking my consent for his union to Ann."

"Oh. Cool. Awesome."

"Yes, it is wonderful news, isn't it?" she says, her gaze passing from me to Alma.

"The best," I reply in what I hope is a convincing tone.

"I am so very pleased for her," Alma adds, sounding almost as insincere as me for some reason.

"He is very rich," Alice chimes in helpfully.

"Quite," Mrs Allander concludes.

Silently this time, she resumes what probably isn't her first read of the letter.

I have an urge to go hide upstairs before remembering that Ann is there. My lungs stop working for a second. If Twain forwarded a letter, it means that Ann has already accepted. I wonder how and when he asked her. If Kenilworth knew and helped him prepare the right words, the ones he'd like to hear if 19th century society wasn't so close-minded. That possibility makes me terribly sad.

Looking down, I try to sort out the thoughts muddled with the dejection and lack of sleep I feel. The others' conversation turns into background noise as I do my best to convince myself that all is fine.

There has to be a solution to all that because there usually is one. I just need to find it. Pushing away useless thoughts and feelings, I focus on what's most urgent and draft a mental list.

First, apologise to Ann for disappearing and scaring her.

Second, tell her to not make this giant mistake of a wedding and to please become my precursor lesbian partner so that we will be mentioned in queer history throughout the years, because that's how awesome we could be together...

I shake my head and pinch the top of my nose, frustrated. This is not working. So I retrace my plan backwards to the only logical part and get my limbs working to rise from the couch.

Step one.

Chapter Thirty

Ann's unmoving form greets me when I enter the room. She's laying on her side of the bed, her back to me and what seems to be my pillow crushed against her.

"I'm sorry I disappeared and scared you," I say, faithful to my decision.

I wait for her snarky reply to counterattack with witty sarcasm, then to fall back in our usual routine of banter and arguments. Except Ann doesn't say a word. She doesn't move. She just lays there, worryingly quiet.

I sit on my side of the bed and reach to poke her shoulder, hoping for a reaction. Then I keep poking until she turns to me, abruptly shoving my hand away. My teasing smile falls.

Ann's eyes are red, blue shadows tinting the bridge of her nose. Her skin is pale, tired. Her hair is dishevelled, a violet ribbon dangling miserably from a strand.

"Oh, Ann..." I whisper sadly.

"No. I do not need your pity," she says, her tone cutting. "You left us there. You left *me*."

"I thought it was for the best," I try helplessly to explain. "I thought that's what you wanted?"

"Why would I ever want such a thing?"

"Because you said time and time again that you don't want me to involve myself in all this marriage business. And it's fine, but that's why I left," I say before remembering something disagreeable that I should do. "By the way..."

"Do not dare congratulate me."

She drops back on her side, but sits up as suddenly, her expression contorted as she glares at me in silence. Sighing, I run a hand through my hair.

"Ann, I just... I don't understand. You and Twain seemed to be an almost sure thing and now, you are. Alma doesn't seem to particularly care for Kenilworth, which is also what you wanted. It all worked out as you expected, so why are you in such a state?"

"Because it isn't all I want!" she explodes.

And she lunges at me, pining me on the bed. And her lips are on mine. Her hand roams on my side before moving up to my hair. I chase her mouth when I feel her tense against me as she seems to realise what's happening. But when she starts to move away, I pass my arm around her back, our bodies colliding.

"No no no," I whisper against her lips, relishing the soft gasp she lets out when I kiss her again, deeply.

Her moment of hesitation is enough for me to take the lead. I sit up, Ann straddling me, her skirts bunched around her knees. I lose my hand in the softness of her hair, removing the forgotten tie without breaking the kiss. The long strands fall freely on her shoulders as I move to bite her neck lightly. When Ann moans at the contact, I nip a little deeper before leaning back. In awe, I stare at her closed eyes, her parted lips, the blush going from her neck to her cheeks...

"Ann," I whisper, afraid to ruin the moment. "Look at me."

And when she does, it's everything. I could feast for years on the desire I read in her eyes. Pressing on her back, I bring her closer, her chest against mine, her arms around my neck. I bury my face against the soft skin of the curve just below her jaw, pushing her sleeve down to kiss my way to her shoulder.

Ann cups my cheek with one hand, bringing my attention back to her face and her heavy-lidded eyes. I feel a radiating smile settling on my face when our lips meet again. Softness turns to longing and impatience, making clear everything we didn't say all those weeks.

"You know how to kiss," I remark, more than a little dazed by the experience. "How?"

"I may not come from the future, but I am not as innocent as you seem to believe me to be," she teases.

"Men or women?" I ask after a second of hesitation, again worried I'll go too far and destroy whatever magic is happening.

But she only chuckles and drops a kiss on the corner of my mouth, her arms tighter around my neck.

"Women. Always women."

I don't hold back my sigh of relief and we laugh together, lips touching, hands exploring.

"Wait. I just... I have so many questions," I say, breaking the kiss once more. "Do you—"

"They will have to wait, just as I waited," Ann interrupts, her lips grazing mine, before confessing. "I would have declared myself to you this past week if you had not insisted on running away. I have wanted to for some time."

"Really? How long have you known I'm gay?" I ask, only realising now how much time we may have wasted.

"Pardon?"

"Ah, right. I'm not sure what term is being used right now, apart from gross ones, but... Gays are homosexuals? People who love people of their own gender?" I explain before realising something else.

"There's so, *so* much I have to tell you! You probably won't believe it all."

But before I can start blowing her mind with all that's been done in the years between us, I focus back on the present.

"But what I meant was, when did you realise I also loved women?"

"I had my suspicions."

"Oh, really? Was it when you saw my modern clothes? My short hair? My lack of 'femininity'?" I tease, a kiss punctuating each sentence.

"Not at all. It was all the looks you turned my way when you thought I was not paying attention. And your clear jealousy towards Jeremiah all but confirmed it."

"Erg, Twain..." I groan at this reminder of the situation existing outside of this room.

"Yes, my future husband," Ann says lightly, playing with a not-so-short-anymore strand of my hair.

"Wait, you just spent about ten minutes kissing me and now you're calling him your husband?"

I start to lean back, which does not work as well as expected because Ann is still straddling me. She tilts her head with a confident smile.

"Believe me when I say you have no reason to worry about Jeremiah."

The cogs in my head start turning and a wave of relief takes over.

"You know, don't you?"

"If you are referring to the fact that Jeremiah and Benedict are, as you say, 'gay', indeed I do. I have from the day we met. They aren't so discreet in the private sphere as they would like to think."

"Quite," I agree, thinking back on that moment in the library. "But you know your... future husband is gay and you still want to go through with it? I'm not sure I understand."

Ann starts to climb away from my lap, which I take as a sign that a serious conversation is about to begin. So I let her, clasping her hand in mine as she sits beside me.

"I cannot say I understand how life is in your own time for people like us. But seeing as you were not surprised and instead quite… responsive," she says with a charming blush, "I can only assume our future is brighter."

I settle somewhere between nodding and shaking my head, a conflicted expression on. She smiles lightly.

"I cannot wait to hear more. But for now, you must know that here, our kind is not talked about. For most people, we do not exist as long as we are not seen. We women are not believed able of such a conduct and so, are forgotten about. But men have been imprisoned, put on trial, deported, executed… Jeremiah and Benedict warned me, with what they have seen and heard in London. For my part, I did not truly believe before meeting them that there were more like me."

I nod not to interrupt. I remember reading about too many queer people in history who said the exact same thing, even years and years from now. But I also wonder what happened with the woman—women?—Ann kissed before me…

"I knew before meeting them that I was different," she continues. "But I settled on the idea that I would marry regardless, that I would become wife to a man I could never love as I should. A life of lies, perhaps, but the only one that seemed possible."

I squeeze her hand, fighting the impulse to drag her back for a kiss, just to see this distraught expression vanish from her face.

"I met Benedict and Jeremiah when I found them embracing in a garden," she recalls, smiling at the memory. "They were so terribly afraid I would tell on them. Me! It was a frightening moment for us all. But soon enough, we came to understand that we were alike in our inclinations, and we became fast friends. They were relieved to have found an ally they could trust, and I was myself happy to learn I was not so alone anymore."

"Is that when the whole wedding idea happened?"

"We did mention it—more as a jest than anything—but yes," she confirms. "Then I could already see what good could come out of it. A rich husband, a name in society, but also relief for my family and close friends by my side for all of our lives. No jealousy or lies between us. We all agreed it was a most perfect plan."

"Was?" I ask with a frown. "What changed?"

Ann scoffs and looks at me with what I now recognise to be a mix of amusement and tenderness.

"You did."

I swallow back a squeal, which would be super not butch of me, and instead drop a kiss on her knuckles.

"You worried me before I even met you and aggravated me from the day I met you," Ann continues. "But every day since, I grew to like you a little more until my affection became irrepressible."

I forgo my butchy side then and laugh shyly.

"In my time, you would have just said you thought I was hot and wanted to kiss me."

"I am not sure what you mean by 'hot', but I did want to kiss you. For a long time now."

"And I'm glad you did…"

Our gazes meet, our want reciprocated, but Ann stops only an inch from my lips with a teasing smile.

"And what would happen next in your time?" she asks in a husky tone that almost makes me swoon.

"I would kiss you back, then we would go home…" I say, running my eyes to where her shoulder is bare thanks to my hard work earlier. "We would fall in bed together…"

"It seems we already have…" Ann whispers back, her eyes devouring my lips.

"Then we would turn off the lights and…" I continue, reaching for the candle.

"Don't," Ann says, the heavy yearning in her voice setting me on fire. "I want to see you…"

When our lips meet again, it's with the same intensity, if not more, than the first time. The night drifts away as we lose ourselves in each other's arms.

Chapter Thirty-One

"Oh dear, it must be quite late already," Ann sighs, shuffling to get out of bed.

Uninterested by anything that isn't a lazy morning in bed with Ann, I pass my arm around her stomach and drag her back to me. Luckily enough, she complies and I'm free to bury my face against her nape, one arm draped over her.

"Is this how you will behave from now on?" she asks, amused, her fingers light on my arm. "Distracting me from my chores with caresses?"

"You kissed me and now I'm going to be awfully needy, yes," I reply, pressing my lips to her cheek. "But in all seriousness, do you actually have to get up?"

She glances at the window. The curtains are half open, bright sunshine bathing the room.

"I believe I should have been downstairs for a little while already," she says before giving me a soft look. "But I doubt a few more minutes in bed will change a thing."

So she settles more comfortably close to me, and I let myself look at her because I can, now. I realised at some point last night that I have wanted this with her for longer than I thought, maybe even from the start. Except I chose not to let myself think about it, refusing the questions that would inevitably come. They try to enter my blissed-out mind now, but I cut short to it. Instead, I focus on Ann's words as she lists all she has to do today.

"What can I do to help?" I ask.

"Well, we are expected at a neighbour's house for tea, but I do not think Alice will want to come. Perhaps the two of you could go for a walk? And I am sure Janet would appreciate the exercise as well."

I stretch lazily then, enjoying the idea of a quiet day with the two girls.

"And..." Ann continues.

She softly drags her fingertips on my arm, a delightful shiver taking hold of me. Interested, I move closer.

"Perhaps we could meet in the garden later? Just you and I? I believe I am long due a gardening lesson."

"Oh, I don't know if that's for you," I tease. "The art of gardening requires rough work. From what I've seen last night, you like softness and nimble fin—"

"I am sure to be an excellent student when I put my mind to it," Ann interrupts with a laugh.

I can still feel her smile when she brings our lips into a kiss, the tingle of anticipation exploding into full-blown desire between us. I have a mind to forget about her duties and to show her what else I've learned in the 21st century, when someone has the *audacity* to knock at the door.

"Ann, are you awake?" we hear Alice shout from the corridor. "Mamma says you repaired my apron? I need it immediately. Janet and I are baking biscuits!"

When Alice tries to open the door, we both roll apart before remembering that Ann thought to lock it yesterday. I look at Ann then, who gathered the bedsheets to hide her bare frame, and let out a chuckle of relief. She gestures at me to be quiet.

"I will only be a moment, Alice," Ann answers, loud enough to be heard through the door.

"Why is your door locked?" the girl continues. "And have you seen Max? I am worried she is hiding somewhere again."

"I am sure she has not gone far," Ann replies evenly.

"Not far at all," I whisper to her with a grin.

Ann chuckles lightly, but stops when our eyes meet. Her gaze then falls to my lips, and I start to reach for her...

"Ann? Did you say something?" Alice asks loudly, trying the handle again.

Not giving me time to react, Ann jumps out of bed. I groan at the disappearance of her warmth against me, but having a full view of the faint marks my teeth left on her skin makes it better.

"I will bring your apron to the kitchen, Alice. Go back to Janet for now," Ann says patiently.

We stay silent until Alice's steps have disappeared down the stairs. Ann looks at me where I'm laying lazily in the bed, the sheet purposefully rumpled to expose my legs and arms. I'm hoping to entice her back to me, but she dresses up quickly. Then, without a second of hesitation, she takes down the sheet behind which we changed until now.

"I do not think there will be a need for that anymore," she says with a delightful grin before exiting the room.

When the door closes, I lay back against the pillows, a silly, wonderful smile settling on my lips still warm with Ann's kisses.

Chapter Thirty-Two

I spend the day walking on thin air, cleverly avoiding all questions from Alice and ignoring her when she mumbles that my bright grin makes me look deranged. Actually, I barely pay attention to anything she and Janet are saying during our walk. That's how besotted and impatient for Ann to come back I am.

There's so much I want to ask and tell her, even more now that my mind has cleared out a little and that I can think more rationally. I want to hear more about how she came to realise she was queer. I want to see her face when I describe the progress made until my century, and the fights won. And maybe later, when we have time, I'll talk about the fights we lost. About the prejudice, the indifference and the violence we faced and are still facing. Maybe later.

For now, I want to focus on the good.

When I see Ann, Alma and Mrs Allander coming towards us at the other end of the path, I restrain myself not to follow Alice when she runs to meet them. As we get closer, Ann's eyes find mine and the smile that appears on her face makes my heart flutter embarrassingly. I press a hand against my chest and Ann's smile widens.

"I trust you had a lovely afternoon?" Mrs Allander asks.

She wraps one arm around Alice, who is chattering rapidly with Alma, exchanging news.

"It was a most refreshing walk, Ma'am'," Janet says with a small curtsy.

"Shall we return to the house together?"

Too busy staring at Ann like a love-struck maiden, I barely hear Mrs Allander's question.

"Max and I are to spend an hour in the garden before dinner, Mother. She meant to teach me the nimble art of gardening," Ann says innocently.

I nearly choke.

"Is it proper for a young lady to—" Mrs Allander starts, but Alice interjects.

"Mamma, you *must* try the biscuits Janet and I made. I want marmalade on mine!"

"Very well, my dear," Mrs Allander says with a smile for her youngest before looking at Ann. "Please be mindful of your dress."

***

We were not mindful of the dress.

Mid-kiss, I praise whatever magic transported me here to have done so just before summer, so that I'm able to frolic in the grass with the woman I adore.

"Tell me more," Ann says, not for the first time.

"Hm, what else... Ah yes, there was—will be—a fantastic American woman living in Paris., a lesbian, like us. Being from a rich family, she was able to be independent and, trust me, she grabbed every opportunity."

"How do you mean 'independent'?"

"I mean that she lived on her own, in her own apartment, doing whatever she wanted. She was a poet, a writer, she published a few books. She was known for her intelligence, her culture, her parties, her long string of female lovers..."

"And the society of her time accepted her?" Ann asks, captivated.

I think for a second.

"I wouldn't go as far as to say she was accepted; it was still—will be—the late 1800s after all. But she didn't care about whatever anyone could have to say about her. And honestly, that's something you find a lot in the queer community of my time."

Ann frowns at the word.

"I'm not going to delve into the etymology of the word for now," I say, "but it's a good word. It has strength. And meaning."

Ann nods, then lies on her back, eyes to the sky.

"Most of what you told me seems impossible and yet... If you said our kind was allowed to marry in your time, I would almost believe it."

I can't help but grin.

"Well, actually..."

She sits right back up at that, eyes wide open.

"It cannot be!"

"It is. Since 2014 for the United Kingdom. So still a while to go from now, but you know. Progress."

Stunned, she looks down at her feet.

"I know a few people who got married over the past few years," I continue. "The parties were nice. Actually, fun fact, but the first sort of recorded lesbian wedding was..."

I stop, realising something.

"Okay, wow. This is insane."

Ann looks at me worryingly.

"Max?"

"I was going to use past tense, but she's alive right now! Like, if I went to Halifax, she could be around. This is... Wow."

"You aren't making any sense?"

I force myself to stop thinking about which other famous people are alive right now, before explaining.

"There's a lesbian alive somewhere right now who's going to inherit some land and money. And at some point in her life, she's going to get sort of married to her female partner, Ann Walker."

I laugh out loud at how ridiculous it is that I'm currently alive at the same time as Gentleman Jack.

"What a wonderful dream it is," Ann sighs.

"It's more than a dream, though."

"For people with means, perhaps. But not all women have the chance to be rich and independent."

Eager to move away from this possibly dangerous territory, I settle the matter with a kiss.

"Let's not think about stuff like that, okay? We should just enjoy the present moment or whatever the correct saying is."

So, Ann only crowds against me, her hand clutching mine, and things couldn't feel more right.

Chapter Thirty-Three

For a couple of weeks, I live in pure bliss. Lost in my own felicity, everything else moves to the background. Although I try not to neglect the rest of the family, I think I get a little lost in my Ann-shaped world.

Ann and I grab every opportunity to be alone during the day, our nights together never enough. Even the unavoidable social visits become our playground as we seize every chance to flirt discreetly. I catch Alma looking at us curiously more than once, but I'm sure that whatever she's imagining can't be close to the truth. After all, this particular truth surely isn't something she could ever imagine.

But too soon, I'm forced to return to reality.

***

Alice finds Ann and I one afternoon, as we're walking back from a solitary trip at the other end of the garden. She's waving a letter above her head, the sight of which makes me inexplicably uneasy.

"Ann, another!" Alice announces cheerfully, handing the envelope to her sister.

Ann glances at me before thanking Alice with a tense smile. She doesn't open the letter, however, instead folding it as if to make it as small as possible.

"It could be important?" I remark.

"I am sure it isn't."

"But—" Alice interjects.

"Alice, please return to the house."

"I want to know what it says!" the girl complains.

"Not now," Ann replies, a little too curtly, maybe because Alice is on the verge of tears.

I feel like I should say something, but Ann seems off and I simply don't like it.

"Hey Alice, we'll follow in a second, alright?"

She throws Ann an irritated look before stomping back to the house. When I turn to Ann again, the letter has disappeared in the pleats of her skirt.

"Okay, what's wrong?"

"Nothing of note," she answers, not meeting my eyes.

"Please don't hide things from me?"

I reach for her hand, and she squeezes mine once before letting go and sighing.

"It is another letter of congratulations. From an acquaintance of Jeremiah's."

"Ah."

It's my turn to look down, thrown out of balance. How stupid is it that I could have forgotten about Twain and this wedding and the fact that Ann couldn't publicly be with me? While we're being careful around the house, here, it feels easy to be together. We can be alone, just the two of us, without anyone truly caring or being suspicious. I sometimes forget that the outside world isn't as forgiving.

"It's going to sound silly, but as we didn't mention it at all lately, I assumed the wedding was... off?" I say, trying to clear my thoughts as I speak.

"Oh, Max... You must know it cannot be..."

"But, uh..." I try, unable to control the pathetic tilt of my tone. "What about us?"

Ann inhales sharply, her words coming out strangled.

"I do not know, Max. I never thought there could be an *us*."

"But there is."

"Yes. But I have also made a promise to Jeremiah."

"Right..."

I rub my temples, scratching them more than anything, as I try to make sense of what all of this means for Ann and for me. For Twain and Kenilworth. For the Allanders.

"It's, uh. It's a lot to process. I honestly don't know where to start."

When I finally manage to meet Ann's eyes, I can read the panic in them. I hurry to grab her hand.

"Oh no, no, please don't look at me like that! I'm not trying to be dramatic, we're not in a Brontë novel. I just suck at dealing with emotions and this is a clusterfuck of emotions. So I just... I might need a moment to wrap my head around it, you know. Do you mind?"

I'm glad to see Ann's signature mix of amusement and exasperation reappear.

"Once again, I did not understand a word—"

"It's a good thing you're so pretty."

She slaps my shoulder, not missing a beat.

"But I will assume I do not need to worry, as you did not run away in the park like the wildling you tend to be."

"Your face is a wildling," I mutter, rubbing my shoulder.

But Ann is already walking towards the house, smiling at me teasingly over her shoulder.

"Again, not a word!"

I look down to hide my silly smile, then leave in the other direction, letting the barrage of my thoughts break open.

***

"I don't like it," I inform Ann a few hours later as I'm joining her in bed.

"I cannot say I do either," she agrees warily, fiddling with the book in her hands.

"But it's the best solution."

She looks up at that, visibly surprised.

"Did you think I was going to make a scene and beg you on my knees not to marry him?" I joke.

"Perhaps not on your knees, but I was expecting some protesting, yes."

"I thought about it, but I have a reputation of cold-hearted monster to maintain."

"Only today, you refused to let go of me until I kissed you good morning."

"Cold-hearted monster!" I repeat with more strength. "But moving on. Sure, I don't like it very much, but I think it's mostly the idea of you being married that doesn't amuse me. But then again, is it really a wedding if it's with Twain?"

"It will be in name. And we will live as a married couple. But only in name."

"Exactly. And I was thinking earlier, I doubt that Twain is going to let go of Kenilworth. So there will be some sort of arrangement between all of you, right?"

"We have not yet discussed the details, but there will be indeed."

"And so..." I start, turning to look at her. "There could be a place for me in that arrangement, do you think?"

"Well, yes, of course," Ann replies with a frown. "But Max..."

"It isn't my time, I know."

"You said you wished to go back?"

"I did, but that was before us. I'm not so sure I want to, now."

Ann simply looks at me as if she was trying to read what was going on in my head. I sigh.

"I don't know exactly what it means to stay here, you know, for the people around me, the life I have there. Will I be instantly erased from everyone's memory from the moment I say I'm staying here? Or will they assume I got kidnapped or something? It's a little scary to think about. And..."

I glance at Ann before continuing.

"I wasn't alone in the gallery that day, when I was brought here. What if she has been searching for me this whole time? What if she's scared and worried because of me?"

Ann gently brushes my hair back, my eyes closing at the sensation.

"I wish I had an answer to your worries," she says, "but as you know, your situation is rather unique. However, I fear I must ask... Is it a risk you are willing to take? Can you live without knowing?"

She continues her caress, her fingertips dragging softly against my forehead each time. I can feel her heart beating faster against my shoulder and I smile, the choice so obvious.

"Yeah. Yeah, I think I can. I know it's a massive decision and it should feel harder to make up my mind, but it really doesn't. You're worth it. Unless... you want me to go?"

My tone might be teasing, but it doesn't mean I'm not absolutely terrified of her answer. Me leaving would be best for Ann. I'm sure we both know it, and I would leave if she asked me to. But I don't know how I would bear it. That explains why relief washes over me at her next words.

"You aren't going anywhere I am not..."

We both know there is much more that should be discussed. But I can see that Ann wants to hang to the possibility that I could stay, that we could be together, as much as I do.

So we don't.

Chapter Thirty-Four

Sprawled on the carpet, Alice and I are studying a map of the world, Fitz swatting at Alice's hand each time she turns a page. Alice uses the map as a general knowledge exercise, but I'm just amazed by it. Some of it seems so wrong to my eyes. I make a mental note to bring the map upstairs tonight, so that I can show Ann all the places I have been to. Hopefully, she'll find my adventures impressive and—

"Ann, there is a letter from M. Twain for you," Mrs Allander announces, taking it out from the pile Janet brought earlier.

As often, my gaze follows Ann as she crosses the room to get the letter, then returns to her chair. She immediately opens it, eyes running along the sentences. When she reaches the end, her mouth twists.

Alarmed, I get up and move behind her chair to read over her shoulder. Halfway through the letter, I make some sort of indecisive grunt. Ann looks up at me, apparently sharing my feelings.

"Is everything well?" Alma asks, her curious gaze on us.

I realise then that I unconsciously laid my hand on Ann's shoulder. I take it back and stretch exaggeratedly which, I'm sure, looks very natural.

"Perfectly, yes," Ann reassures her sister. "M. Twain invites me to Squareshaw Park from next week to discuss wedding arrangements."

"Am I to come as well?" Alma asks, visibly eager for some entertainment.

"Not this time, I am afraid..." Ann says after a second of hesitation that only I seem to notice. "But it is only for a week and sure to be quite uninteresting for you."

Frowning, I look down at the carpet. Twain's invitation did include Alma. I wonder why Ann doesn't want her to join.

"M. Kenilworth has added a few lines to extend the invitation to Max, however," she continues in a casual tone. "He mentioned some time ago that he would like to paint us two and it seems he needs us to pose to complete his sketch. And as I require a chaperone, Max will do perfectly."

I look everywhere but at Alma or Mrs Allander, hoping the latter won't contest the plan. To my relief, she only nods.

"Perhaps we could visit you in a few days," she says. "It would do us all good to enjoy the summer breeze."

"I will write to M. Twain this instant and make sure to add a line in this regard, Mother."

As Ann leaves the room, I swallow my usual regret that I can't simply touch her hand or say something flirty. Apparently, that's something I like to do now.

But then, with an ecstatic smile, I realise why Ann excluded Alma on purpose.

It will only be the two of us—plus Twain and Kenilworth, I guess—in a giant house for days on end.

Chapter Thirty-Five

Seeing the house for the second time—and knowing what I know now—I don't let myself be impressed.

Okay, maybe just a little. But I'm allowed; it's basically a palace.

We go through the usual bowing and general polite stuff in front of the house, in the presence of the staff. For once, I comply because Ann asked me to. Then, we retreat inside, in one of the rooms reserved for our private use. Twain explains that, to not disturb the wedding preparations, the staff had been limited to a few people of trust and the neighbours have not been warned of our presence.

When we enter what I recognise to be the library, I obviously snicker at the memory I associate with it. The two men invite us to settle, but instead of aiming for the solo seat by the empty chimney, I sit very close to Ann on the small couch she claimed obviously on purpose.

Right after Ann accepted the invitation, I asked her if she told the two men about us. She replied that she didn't feel comfortable writing it down in a letter that could be read, which is understandable. So witnessing the men's surprise is delightful, even more so when Ann casually takes my hand in hers.

Kenilworth is the first to recover.

"Well now. It seems we are entirely amongst same-minded people," he says, his hand finding Twain's shoulder.

The latter is still staring, mouth agape.

"What, you didn't think women could also be together?" I tease him.

"Of course I did," he protests, coming back to himself. "Only... I did not think Ann could be interested in... Well, in you."

"Okay? I'm not sure how to take that."

"Are you certain it is wise?" he asks Ann, ignoring me.

"I don't think I like him very much," I note to no one in particular, more than a little annoyed.

"I couldn't be surer," Ann declares, which puts a stop to the matter for now.

She adds a little distance between us when the maid knocks, then comes in with tea. I settle on throwing daggers at Twain, who immediately frowns, arms crossed.

***

The following day makes it clear that Twain's nice personality is only a façade. At least when it comes to me. Kenilworth doesn't seem too surprised by it; Ann is distracted.

Twain ignores my presence whenever he can. He scoffs at my affectionate gestures towards Ann and even goes as far as to try to keep me away from Kenilworth. The latter pays him no mind, however—which irritates Twain and entertains me—as he started working on his sketch. And well, I happen to be a major component of it.

Now that I have decided to stay, I doubted the need for the portrait. But when debating it with Ann the evening before our arrival, she made a good point. It needs to exist or it could change the course of the future. After all, if I didn't see and touch it, I wouldn't be here right now.

The thought that a simple painting—and myself by extension—could have an impact on the future is more than a little scary. And knowing that when the portrait is finished, even grazing it could be enough to send me forward, is not something I'm comfortable with.

Maybe that's why I don't say anything when the sketch Kenilworth shows us is all wrong.

Ann shared with him the details I told her weeks before—the chair, the colours of the dresses, the black lines on my wrist—which he added. But the general aspect of it, the positions, the room, the expressions... None of it is right.

Whatever he ends up producing won't be *our* painting.

Before I can convince myself that saying something is the right thing to do, Kenilworth adds the final touch to his drawing and Ann turns to me with a serene smile. I force myself to smile back, not quite meeting her eyes.

***

After that, what I expected to be a lovely escapade with Ann in a fancy house turns into a wedding planning marathon.

Ann and Twain spend hours perfecting the details, from who to invite to the ceremony to ideas for how we will all live afterwards. The future bridegroom is rather disgruntled to now have to include me.

One afternoon, I offer to help, but Twain hides scribbled documents under his hands like a petulant child, as if I was trying to steal his secrets. I roll my eyes and leave for the garden, hoping for a distraction, which comes in the form of Kenilworth reading a book on a bench. I drop next to him with a heavy sigh.

"Is Twain always so annoying?"

"He is simply quite busy," Kenilworth answers in a neutral tone. "His temper can take a bad turn in situations such as this."

"I don't understand how you can stand him. You're so..."

I look at him, his hands gently resting over the book on his lap, his expression soft and relaxed. When we met, I thought him to be overly jovial and too friendly, but from the day we arrived here, I realised it was only an act. The real Kenilworth is clear-headed, thoughtful and temperate. I had to revise what I thought I knew about him and am glad of it.

"Yes?"

"You're calm and mild while Twain is an irritating bundle of nerves."

He laughs at that.

"It does describe him well enough indeed. But surely, you understand it is only because of the situation we find ourselves in."

"The wedding, you mean?" I sigh, letting my irritation about Twain bubble up. "It doesn't annoy you to be carted aside?"

Kenilworth smiles slightly, thinking for a second.

"This scheme, for the lack of a better word, we are attempting all rests on Ann and Jeremiah. They will be the ones scrutinised relentlessly. They not only put themselves in danger by associating with us but also their family. They risk losing everything. While us..."

He studies my face for a moment before continuing.

"Pardon me if my assumptions are incorrect, but I believe we are equals in that Ann is the most important person in your eyes, if not the only one. As Jeremiah is for me. If there were to be a rumour or an accusation, they both would be wise to move away from us and to settle in their matrimonial life, regardless of how insincere it is. They would lose us, yes, but they would keep their families, their reputation, their place in society."

As he pauses, I wonder how long he's been thinking about all this. How much it has weighed on him.

"I understand that Ann and yourself have not been thus associated for long," he continues. "Myself, I have been by Jeremiah's side for almost six years. I know how easier his life would be if he would simply forget about me and his inclinations, and settle in what is considered a normal life."

"You can't mean that..."

"I do. I suppose that what I am trying to say, with difficulties, is that yes, I do dislike our current situation. I dislike that Jeremiah feels under constant pressure, even now that we have a chance to be together away from society for some time. Our life in London has never been easy. We have had to maintain pretences for years and to always be careful, which causes a strain on us both. As such, while I have noticed that he has been discourteous towards you since your arrival, I fear he only sees you as one more threat that could arise."

"I would never—"

"I know this, I do, because you and I are in the same position," he says, squeezing my hand. "But while I would like for us all to be able to live freely without having to concern ourselves with the opinion of others, it is not to be. So yes, I do dislike this situation and being carted aside, as you so rightly put. Yet I also know that Ann and Jeremiah have our best interests in mind. It is because they love us that they are willing to bear so many lies and trials. I chose long ago to stay at his side as long as he will have me. If bearing his temporary bad temper is what I need to do to be with him until the end, I will gladly do so."

I nod weakly, thoughts swirling in my head.

"But... What about your own reputation? Surely you have as much to lose?"

"Ah well," Kenilworth replies with an amused smile.

His accent loses its refinement then, the vowels sounding rougher, some consonants swallowed.

"It is possible I am not the gentleman I pretend to be."

I stare at him, stunned.

"My father was a simple merchant from Liverpool, and I grew up as a merchant's son would, neither rich nor poor. When I was discovered to have a good eye for art, I was given the opportunity to change the course of my life."

"That's how you met Twain?"

"Indeed. I became an apprentice to a London artist, who was then asked to paint the Twains' family portrait. I went to assist him..."

"And the rest is history," I say with a smile.

"I suppose we could say that, yes. I worked hard to elevate in society and to be worthy of being considered Jeremiah's close friend. Most of my upper-class acquaintances know nothing of my origins because I would never endanger my relationship with the man I love."

I can't help but grin at him then, proud that he finds me deserving of his trust.

"Okay then. I'll do my best to ignore Twain when he's being annoying. But only because you made a compelling argument," I say, making him laugh.

"Your efforts are greatly appreciated."

Chapter Thirty-Six

I make good on my promise to be more patient with Twain as soon as the following morning. Even though he kept Ann up until late in the night. And even though he just finished the last of the tea as I was reaching for it, actually smirking evilly at me. When I glance at Benedict, annoyed, he offers no help, only covering an amused grin with his hand.

Allowing myself one glare at Twain, I push my chair away from the table and get up.

"Just going to the kitchen for some tea," I say to answer Ann's wondering look.

But I have barely stepped into the corridor that one of the maids barrels into me, leaving me just the time to catch her before she falls.

"Is everything okay?" I ask, noticing her red cheeks and wide-eyed look.

"The Endowe family is at the gate!"

"I thought no one knew we were here?"

"It seems the kitchen boy could not hold his tongue at the market!"

"Great."

I step back to the door and raise my voice so that the others can hear me.

"Hey, I think we have a small problem. There's an Endowe family currently on their way to the door?"

A few seconds of perfect stillness, then chaos. They all lunge to their feet to start gathering flying pages, pens, and legal books in a hurry. Benedict forces Twain to let him clear up the rest and to go get changed. Ann rushes to the door, grabs my hand, and we run upstairs to put on more appropriate clothes.

By the time we come down, everyone is settled in the parlour, conversing politely. Two kids are playing on the carpet a little further. Once we've been introduced, Ann whispers to me that I can go play with them if I like. I answer with a vexed look.

"Why would I? I hate kids. Also, I'm old enough to listen to an adult conversation, you know."

"As you seem to adore my sister, I assumed it was the same with all children. And I know you are. I only wish to spare you."

"Your sister's great, so that's different. But help appreciated."

I reach to arrange the shawl on her shoulders, answering her smile with one of my own.

Eventually, the unwelcomed neighbours leave. My relief is cut short, however, when Twain intercepts me as I'm going upstairs and asks me coldly to join him in the library.

Somehow, I doubt he wants literary advice.

***

"How can you be so irresponsible!" he all but yells at me.

"Wow, calm down, cowboy," I answer with a nervous chuckle. "What's going on?"

"How do you not understand that any affectionate word or gesture, even the most subtle, can appear suspect to others?"

I frown at him until I understand what he may be talking about.

"Is it because I helped Ann with her shawl earlier? I barely touched her!"

"Even a blind man could see the affection between the two of you!"

"You're exaggerating."

Twain starts pacing around the room, hands shaking. And that's when I realise something. He's not angry. He's scared.

I take a few steps towards him, my hands raised in a peace attempt.

"Hey, look at me..."

When he does, I lead him to a chair and wait until his breathing sounds more controlled.

"I'm sorry if what I did seemed suspect—"

"That is just the problem, you see," he interrupts. "You may think it *seemed* suspect, but to the rest of us, it was. Imagine if I acted as you did towards Benedict, imagine how it would appear to others!"

"Maybe you should stop worrying so much about what others think. It's making you a little paranoid," I scoff, annoyed to be reprimanded like a child.

"Do you truly believe I have a choice?" he explodes, standing up. "My life and Jeremiah's depend on it! Ann's as well! You are the only one who does not see all that we are risking!"

"I do," I protest. "Ann told me—"

"Did she tell you about Martin Willoughby, who was hung and left to rot in the sun with a sign accusing him of buggery around his neck? About Clarence Wills, who lost his family and was forced to exile, left to die in poverty?" he screeches, his voice breaking. "From the day we met, you acted recklessly time and time again without a care for your reputation. But you must realise it isn't only your own reputation now! If our arrangement is to work, you need to learn how to behave for Ann's sake. For mine and Benedict's!"

"I'm not a wild animal that needs to be tamed!"

"Then prove it!"

We stare each other down, both breathless. He looks away first.

"I received word today that my parents are to join us the day after tomorrow. If you wish to stay by Ann's side, you need to act accordingly."

"And what does that mean, exactly? Curtsy prettily, make small talk, smile, and nod like I don't have a working mind?"

"If that is what you need to do to appear proper, then yes!"

He drops down on the seat, head in his hands.

I should be angry about the insults he threw at me, but a too large part of me knows he's right. So I run a hand through my hair, pushing it away from my face, and close my eyes for a brief second to calm myself.

"I'm sorry," I let out painfully. "I don't always know how things work here. Or more like, I don't always understand it."

Or agree with it.

"But... Benedict said to me that if bearing some difficulties was what he needed to do to stay with you, he would. And I would do the same for Ann, as long as needed."

"Does it mean I can trust you to meet my parents?" Twain asks, exhaustion roughing his voice.

"I don't know," I answer truthfully. "But I'll figure something out."

Chapter
Thirty-Seven

The following day, I get up before Ann, sneak back to my room—where I haven't slept once, but maybe that should also change—and dress with more care than usual. The staff seems a little surprised to find me sitting quietly at the breakfast table, instead of pillaging the kitchen for scones as I did since my arrival.

When Twain and Benedict enter, I nod politely, asking them if they slept well. Though Benedict seems confused by my behaviour, Twain answers with the same propriety. We leave it there until Ann arrives. I sit still when she kisses me on the cheek. My hands are tightly clasped on my lap to refrain from wrapping my arms around her as my instinct urges me to.

I barely slept all night, turning Twain's words over and over in my head. He was right to say that I acted with a complete lack of awareness since I got here. The Allanders seemed to take my weirdness in stride and learned to get used to it, so I never really gave it a thought, but now...

Looking back, I remember the stunned looks I ignored during my few social outings. I remember Mrs Allander's gentle insistence that I stay home with Alice. I remember Alma's curious, maybe even suspect, glances at my closeness with Ann. How many times did I put them all in danger? How is it possible that it took a man's reproach for me to realise how irresponsible I have been?

The only thing I was sure of when morning came is that I couldn't go on as I did. Benedict changed who he was to be with Twain, and now it seemed it was my turn.

So during breakfast, I stay mostly quiet, only answering when asked something directly. I practice not looking at Ann as much and keeping our private conversation to a minimum. I don't touch her, not even when she lays her hand on mine to ask if I feel fine.

As the hours pass, Ann visibly grows worried, but I ignore it. I force myself to sit still during the whole duration of tea, when I would normally buzz around the room. What I take to be a satisfied nod from Twain is my reward.

By dinner, I feel ill and not only because of the corset I've asked the maid to tie properly this morning. My chest feels constricted, my throat dry. There's the worrying pressure of tears in my eyes. Standing up from my chair at the table, I excuse myself before calmly exiting the room.

Once alone, I rush upstairs to my room, lock the door behind me and sit against the wall, head down, unable to breathe. I may be having a panic attack. It sure feels like one. And if I had to guess, I would say it's related to the slow realization that this is who I have to be if I want to stay. Nothing but a quiet companion with impeccable manners.

Ann and I will never be able to truly be together because we'll never be allowed to show who we are to each other. I don't even care that she's going to marry Twain at this point. Whether she does or not, it won't change a thing for us.

Benedict seems to expect more freedom to result from this wedding; I doubt it'll come to be. One look at the future happy couple's calendar is enough to see that they will be busy for the next few months. And none of those plans include Benedict or me.

For a moment, I let myself imagine how it could be if I had met Ann in my own time. We would walk hand in hand in the street, not caring about who saw us. Hell, we probably would have moved in together by now. It would be easy and normal. Accepted. Not something to be hidden and ashamed of.

A soft knock on the door interrupts the miserable turn of my thoughts. I wipe the tears on my cheeks and sniff inelegantly—a little vengeance against Twain—before getting up to unlock it.

"Max!" Ann exclaims, panicked by the rare sight of my red eyes. "What is wrong?"

"It's nothing. Sorry I left."

"Please do not hide things from me?" she says, opening her arms.

And just like that, my resolution crumbles. I let her hold me tight for what feels like both an eternity and not long enough. A few fresh tears roll from my eyes to her shoulder.

"Don't steal my words, it's not fair game," I mumble against the fabric of her dress.

"You stole my heart. I can steal your words."

At that, I lean back from her embrace with a repulsed groan.

"Okay, no, that was awful. End of hug. Please don't ever say something that sappy again."

Ann walks towards the bed, dragging me after her by the sleeve.

"It seems it was enough to bring back your normal self. I can hardly regret it."

We lay down side by side. Gently, Ann pushes a strand away from my eyes.

"Will you tell me what is wrong now?"

"It's just—It's so stupid," I groan, hiding my face.

"Max…"

I stay silent a little longer, finding some relief in the sensation of her hand smoothing my hair back.

"I had a conversation with Twain yesterday—"

"Did he upset you?" she asks immediately.

"No! Well, yes. But he was right to!" I add when her expression turns thunderous. "Nothing he said wasn't true. I need to be smarter if I want to stay. For you and your family. I've just been impulsive and careless since I arrived, I've put you all in danger."

"Is this the reason why you were an incredible bore today?"

"Hey! I wasn't boring! Was I? Wait, don't answer that," I say, pressing a hand against her mouth.

She pushes my hand away with a chuckle and waits until I dare to look at her. The intensity in her eyes is almost too much for me to bear.

"Whatever Jeremiah told you, it probably was something he felt should be said. But I cannot—I will not ask you to change for me. I love you as you are, Max."

How my tiny messed-up heart lurches at that. When Ann takes my hands in hers, I look down, trying to control the blinding smile I can feel coming.

"You know no one ever said that to me before?"

"I hope it is even more precious to you, then."

"Precious? That's not the word for it, no…"

I frown, thinking.

"It's… nice."

Ann stares at me for a whole minute before speaking again.

"'Nice'? Your answer to my declaration of love is that it is 'nice'?" she says in mock indignation, turning away from me. "Unacceptable. Let us forget about the plan. Please return to your own time."

I pass my arms around her middle to bring her against me, her back to my chest, and hold her there.

"It's nice because hearing you say those words gives me this tingly feeling that warms me up from head to toe," I whisper in her ear, feeling less self-conscious now that our eyes don't meet. "It's nice because I can already imagine hearing those words from you again and again, even when I annoy you and especially when I make you laugh. And it's nice because I... I also love you..."

My voice dies a little at the words that leave my mouth. I rush to say what I need to before my eyes betray me again with tears.

"I just love you so much it's actually ridiculous."

Ann turns in my arms until we're face to face, then kisses me full on the mouth, never hesitating.

"I never thought I would meet the person meant for me..." she whispers, her voice heavy with all sorts of emotions I'm pretty sure we're sharing.

"And I never thought it would take coming to the 19th century to fall in love," I joke, my eyes definitively a little wet. "But..."

Her hand stills on my cheek.

"Max?"

"It's because I love you that I think I should take a step back until the wedding," I explain, unable to hold her gaze.

"Max..."

"I don't want you to think I'm running away or that I'm against all this marriage thing, because again, I'm not. It's far from perfect and I don't know when I'll wrap my head around it, but I promise I will. But I also don't want to have to change because I don't know that I can."

"I do not wish you to."

"I know. I know... It's just... I want us to be together. But I don't know how to pretend you're nothing more than a friend to me when I'm mad about you."

"What do you propose, then?" she asks, sounding a little worried.

"Honestly, I don't know yet," I sigh. "My plan for today clearly didn't work. I don't think my act convinced anyone."

"Well, it may have till you let Jeremiah read aloud from *Candide* without a complaint."

"Ah, don't remind me, that was awful," I groan. "It's so boring! And the man read it in its original French! Could he be more pretentious?"

"Ah, there you are," Ann says with a tender smile.

I shuffle closer, needily, her arms tightening around me.

"I think I should go home for now. To your home, I mean," I correct myself.

"I believe my family would agree with me to say it is also yours."

It takes me a second to answer as this yet unexplored possibility makes its way into my brain. I can't help the pleased smile that curves my lips.

"I'll go home then. To our home," I say, the words enough to give me a new sort of hope. "I think it's best that I avoid Twain's family. I don't want to risk any unnecessary drama."

We stay wrapped in each other for a moment, both silent.

"I dread being parted from you," Ann confesses.

"It's not for long though, right? You'll be back soon enough, with a perfectly planned scheme for our future."

She thinks for a moment, but I know she will also see it's for the best.

"I will return home as soon as I can be freed of my obligations," she promises.

"You know I'll be waiting."

Chapter Thirty-Eight

When I step out of the carriage, it feels like months have passed, though it has only been a few days. Not having Ann by my side is unsettling, but I know I need to get used to it, even just a little.

It helps that the rest of the Allanders and Janet seem genuinely happy—if surprised—to see me back so soon. Worried, they ask for news of Ann, then of the two men. I reassure them immediately, joking that I only wished to escape meeting more insufferable rich people.

Which is only half a lie, really.

The routine we settle in then reminds me of the time before Ann arrived. Once again, I spend hours with Alice, trying everything that pops into her mind: baking all sorts of things, theatrical readings, made-up games... I turn out to be bad at most, but Alice never seems to care.

There's one new development that intrigues me, however. I notice that Alma seems to spend a lot of time receiving and writing letters, always with a private smile. It feels like something important has happened in the few days I was away. Even more so when Mrs Allander takes Alma aside one evening, the two of them conferring in low voices and going over one of the letters.

Not wanting to intrude, I leave for the kitchen, hoping to find some answers. Janet is there, decorating a cake for Alice's birthday the next day.

"Do you know what's going on with Alma?" I ask her.

I'm wondering how to steal one of the biscuits she's using for the cake without her realising. They're just here, under my nose. She must know it's tempting.

"Oh, it isn't my place to speak of such matters," she says, immediately blushing.

Sensing her distraction, I make a try for the biscuit. She slaps my hand with a glare. I sit back sadly, but grin when she hands me a discarded one from her last batch.

"You only had to ask."

"Don't try to change the subject," I reply, crumbles falling from my mouth to the table.

When I swipe them away, Janet looks like she wishes for nothing more than my swift death, but sighs and lowers her voice.

"I believe that soon enough, we will learn that Miss Alma is engaged."

I immediately choke on the buttery wonder in my mouth and cough roughly.

"She's what now?" I let out in a strangled voice.

"Please be quiet!" Janet begs. She pats my back until I can breathe normally again before continuing. "I only know because I have heard a conversation between Miss Alma and her mother that was not meant for my ears. I am ashamed to know such a secret..."

"You have as much the right to know as any of us. But wow. Alma engaged..."

A crucial missing element comes to my mind then.

"But wait, to who?"

"Of that, I am not quite sure," Janet frowns. "A gentleman I believe she met at M. Twain's and M. Kenilworth's ball."

"Oh? Ooh!"

I have a vague recollection of the man that seemed so taken with Alma then, but can't seem to remember his face clearly. Maybe I would have paid more attention to him if not for Ann's presence.

"He has been sending several letters each week since the ball and Miss Alma always seems pleased to receive them."

I nibble distractedly on my biscuit, once again fascinated by how much I don't see when Ann is around.

"He better be good enough for her..."

***

Alice made sure to remind me every day since my return that her birthday was coming up. And now that the day has arrived, I have the pleasure to be dragged from sleep by a mass crashing down on me.

Impervious to my panic at being waken up so abruptly, Alice jumps up and down on the bed, singing "My birthday is today, my birthday is today!". And while I appreciate the rime, I'm not sure it's necessary that early in the morning.

Obviously, Alice doesn't grant me a moment to start my brain. Depriving me of my warm and comfortable bed, she forces me to follow her down to the kitchen, where Mrs Allander, Alma, and Janet are already gathered. Two of them look as haggard as I feel.

Mustering as much enthusiasm as possible in the present circumstances, we wish a happy birthday to Alice. She wiggles gleefully in front of her cake, Fitz circling on the floor, waiting for his share.

Finally, once she had a slice—or three—she authorizes us to go dress before whatever mayhem she has planned next.

Mrs Allander and Alma betray me by making up some chores, leaving me at Alice's mercy. By lunch time, when I crumble on the ground, out of breath, I wish I had thought to hide myself in the deepest part of the garden the night before.

"You... win..." I struggle to say.

Alice bounces around me, animated by the vitality of the 13 years old she now is. I lay down completely, the rest of my strength deserting me. Alice looks a little disappointed, but luckily for me, Janet brings her a letter, which helps to distract her.

"Oh Max, look! Ann wrote to me! A whole letter, just for me!" the girl exclaims, ripping the envelope open.

Discreetly, Janet hands me a second letter while Alice is focused on hers, lips moving as she reads. My heart rushes at the familiar writing on the back of the envelope. Unable to wait any longer, I tell Alice I need some water and follow Janet back to the kitchen.

Sitting on the bench, my back turned to Janet, I start to read voraciously. When I reach the end of the letter, I fold it back slowly and slip it in my pocket. It's only then that I notice Janet waiting close with a cup of water.

"Oh. Thanks."

"I trust Miss Ann is well?"

"Yes, she seems fine. But she has to delay her return again. She doesn't know when she'll be back."

I take a sip of water, dejectedly.

"You miss her, do you not?" Janet asks softly.

"So bad."

And I immediately look up, realising what I let out in my distraction.

"We all do, of course," I add quickly, trying to correct my mistake. "It's a shame she's not here for Alice's birthday, also."

Janet doesn't answer, only nodding casually. I study her calm expression a little longer, trying to evaluate how much I messed up, when she speaks again.

"If I were to share a secret with you... Could you promise to keep it?"

That's not what I expected.

"Well, yeah, sure. Of course."

She gestures at me to follow and takes me to a part of the house I never felt right going to before. As we enter her bedroom, I feel a slight sense of discomfort tugging at me, but quickly repress it.

Instead, I look around, amazed by how Janet managed to make the room so completely hers. I spot a few letters—from her family maybe—on a small table by the bed, but also recipe books and even a few novels I recognise from the library.

And something much more surprising.

Flying pages hung on the walls or piled by the bed, sharp lines traced by a skilful hand on thick cream paper. I recognise Alma and Mrs Allander. Alice and I crouching in the garden. Ann reading on her favourite chair... I turn to look at Janet, the question on my lips forgotten when I find her standing by a paint-splattered sheet.

"What's that?" I ask instead.

"It is what I would like to keep a secret. Please, you must promise you will not tell Mrs Allander. I do not wish for her to think I am ungrateful."

"I promise," I say, one hand up, the other on my heart, aware that the significance of the gesture will elude her. "But I'm getting a little worried..."

So she removes the sheet, gathering it against her chest. Stunned, I freeze and stare stupidly at what she revealed.

"I do not think it perfect, far from it... But Miss Alma has taught me what she knows and thinks I have progressed," Janet says, embarrassed, words flying from her mouth. "I know it isn't respectable as I am but a simple maid. I am afraid of what Mrs Allander would think if she ever were to learn about this..."

She looks up at me, hopeful and scared, wrenching her hands.

"Miss Alma said I could trust you if I thought the time was right. And as you seemed to long for Miss Ann, I assumed..."

I slam a hand against my mouth to stop the sob from coming out. I never cried so much before coming here. Feelings are weird.

"Janet, this is... It's *it*. It's the portrait."

"Beg your pardon, Miss?" she answers, confused.

I try to clear my thoughts, my eyes unable to detach from the painting in front of me.

"You did this?"

"Yes. Well, Miss Alma advised me. It was her who thought of the colours of the dresses and the positions. And she was kind enough to lend me her brushes and colours, but I promised to—"

Too quickly for her to react, I trap her in a hug. After a few seconds of hesitation, she rests her hands on my back, though shyly.

"It's wonderful, Janet. It's... It's so beautiful!"

"Oh, Miss!"

I break the embrace, keeping one arm around her shoulders as we both study the painting. It's exactly how I remember it. The imperfections making it perfect. The shades of Ann's skin, the glint in her eyes, our hands brushing near her shoulder. The expression on my half-hidden face as I look at Ann doesn't seem so unbelievable to me anymore. It's love and affection and tenderness, all mixed in the blue of my eyes.

I glance at Janet, surprised to find her gaze already on me and even more to read in it that somehow she knows. She knows about Ann and me. And the painting might just be her way of showing that she doesn't mind. I can see she's struggling to find the words, but I smile and squeeze her hand, letting her know how much it means.

Until I realise something else.

"You said Alma gave you helped you... Has she seen the final result?"

"She was the first to. She said it couldn't be more faithful," Janet confirms before adding in a quieter voice. "In every aspect."

Right.

I push back the inevitability of a conversation with Alma to the back of my mind for now.

"I know I shouldn't ask you that," I hesitate, "but would you mind if I was the one to tell Ann about it when she's back?"

Janet agrees with a smile. We stay in front of the canvas, standing close enough to admire it as it deserves. But far enough so that I can repress this uneasiness that got stronger since I entered the room. The tug that now beckons me *towards* the painting. I take a step back as if it could be enough and fight the impulse to rush out of the room.

"Miss Max?" Janet says with a worried look. "Are you upset?"

I force myself to smile and squeeze her shoulder.

"No, of course not. Thank you for showing me. But, hm... I think Mrs Allander was looking for you earlier," I lie, a little ashamed to.

As I hoped, that's enough to make Janet quickly exit the room and disappear in the corridor. I spare one last glance at the painting before turning my back to it, the threads between us stretching as I walk away.

Chapter Thirty-Nine

Another day, another letter. Ann informs us that when the moment came for Twain's parents to return home, they thought unacceptable that Ann would be left alone with two men, especially if one is her fiancé. So Ann and Twain were both invited to relocate at their estate near Kingston. I spare a thought for Benedict, wondering where he is now.

In a private letter to me, Ann regrets that the invitation was impossible to decline and makes fun of the ridiculousness of M. and Mrs Twain's upper-class attitude, possibly hoping that it would make me laugh. It only deepens how much I miss her.

As with all her letters, I fold it carefully and put it away in my pocket for now, then retreat back to the house after a long walk in the surrounding fields, spent sadly reminiscing about how wonderful it was to have Ann always close.

As I reach the parlour, I spot Alma alone there, sitting comfortably in the chair, reading yet another letter with a smile. I lean against the door, waiting for her to notice me, and clear my throat when she doesn't. Or pretends not to? I know we haven't really spoken just the two of us since I returned. I guess we've both been busy and... It's possible I've avoided her a little too, since Janet showed me the painting. But, as I've learned with Ann months ago, there's no point trying to delay because the moment will come when I won't be able to hide anymore. And well. There's no time like the present.

"So... Rumour has it you're about to get married?"

Alma doesn't even look up from her letter, but I can see the smile on her lips widening.

"You must realise it is a terrible way to engage in a conversation."

"Humour me a little. I'm bored."

"Ah. Of course."

Finally, she looks at me and I do my best to empty my expression of all sad feelings.

"I am sure Ann will come home sooner than we think. She seems quite impatient to return. I wonder why that could be..." Alma remarks neutrally before focusing on her letter once more.

Squinting at her, not amused, I step into the room and stroll casually, hands folded behind my back.

"So... Who sent you that letter?" I ask, hoping to return the favour of entertaining myself with her affections.

She doesn't take the bait, so I continue.

"Could it possibly be a tall man with broad shoulders, a brooding expression and, if my memory is correct... black hair?"

"Brown hair," Alma answers distractedly before realising the trick and glaring at me.

She scoffs at my victorious smile but capitulates, anyway.

"Very well. I might as well tell you now, as it will not stay a secret for long. I am engaged."

I knew it—sort of—but hearing it still surprises me.

"So it's actually really official?"

"Yes. It is actually really official," she repeats, amused.

"And you're... happy about it?" I tread carefully.

She glances down at the letter, then at me. I can't help but smile at the blush colouring her cheeks.

"I am, yes," she confirms with a quiet confidence. "And I have you to thank for this."

"How so?" I ask, puzzled. "I'm known for creating chaos, not for being helpful. Ask your mum. And Janet. And Lady Cuttingham."

"You may be prone to it, yes, but I do not know how our family could be without you. Truthfully, I hardly remember how we were before you came to us. You have changed it all."

I should have a funny remark to contribute, but no. I am struck silent by her sincerity. The question is now: am I going to cry again?

"I believe that, if you had not set an example I wished to follow, I would not have taken the time to get to know M. White as I do now. Though his appearance and manners can seem prickly at first, he has a gentle heart," Alma says, her tone coated with affection. "First impressions are often not to be trusted, wouldn't you agree?"

I scowl a little at her, not impressed by her teasing.

"Sure, but I was hardly prickly at the beginning. A little rude, maybe, but prickly?"

"I never said *you* were."

As the meaning behind her words finally reaches my brain, it's my turn to blush profusely. This constant roller-coaster of emotions would be exhausting if it wasn't so worth it.

Chapter Forty

Since Ann's last letter, where she promised to be back within two weeks, we received little to no news from her. With every new day, it becomes harder to fight the impulse to rush to whatever castle the Twain family lives in and to get Ann back to where she belongs, with us all. But mainly with me.

Finally, on the morning of the last day, a letter.

While we became frequent pen pals since my stay with them—expressing in coded sentences our shared woe—I have never been so unhappy to recognise Benedict's handwriting. He informs me that he has visited Twain and Ann but did not stay long. Twain's parents were not particularly welcoming or bearable, it seems.

So he asks for the pleasure of coming to see me and the Allanders as soon as my answer will reach him. I scribble a positive reply right after consulting Mrs Allander. She seems happy enough to receive him, even though she holds no special interest in him anymore.

On my way out to hand my letter to the messenger who brought Benedict's, I catch a glance of Alma talking and laughing quietly with her now official fiancé. Corny as it may be, seeing her that happy makes *me* happy. When I return from the gate, my letter dispatched, I find Alice peeking through the window, and gesture at her to leave the couple alone.

"But I am bored!" she complains.

"Give me ten minutes and we'll go do something. Except running or climbing," I warn as excitement begins to brighten her face. "Be considerate of my old bones."

Back inside, I chuckle affectionately when I hear Alice start a backward count from ten minutes, then slowly make my way upstairs. As I reach the landing, I hesitate, once again dreading the moment when I'm in our room but Ann isn't. I've tried to accept that she was stuck and that she enjoyed it as little as I did. But as the weeks passed, it became more and more difficult to stay tolerant of the situation.

The image I created in my mind back at Twain's, of Ann and I living together openly, came back to me often, details adding to it against my will. I started planning the moment when I would show her Janet's painting and ask her if she could also feel the pull. And she would be confused, but she would say that yes, she did. And then, she would look at me and together, we would press our hands against the canvas and...

I shake my head, irritated at myself for straying too far into fantasy again. Even if she did feel anything, Ann wouldn't leave here, not even for me. I get it because I also love her family and I know it would crush her to never see them again. Still, my selfish need to have her all for myself rears its ugly head, stifling everything else.

The pull of the portrait feels sharper than it ever had until now as the thought makes its way. Our painted image engraves itself into my mind once more. It calls to me. And although I'm quite sure I don't want to go back and lose everything I found here, the loneliness I felt those past weeks without Ann makes it harder to resist.

I just want to see her.

Before even realising it, I'm knocking at Janet's door and pushing it open when only silence answers me. Though uncomfortable at being here without her, I notice that a corner of the sheet is hanging low, showing the mass of hair at the back of my head. The pull irrepressible now, I enter the room and close the door, moving quietly.

A light tug is enough to make the sheet cascade down to the ground, pooling at my feet. I let my eyes wander hungrily across the canvas as I hunt for details yet unnoticed, avoiding stopping on myself for too long.

I know I have been scared of that painting, of what it represents. I sure did my best to avoid it until now. Janet and Alma haven't mentioned it to me, nor I to them, and we simply pretended it wasn't here.

Except being left to think about something over and over in your own head is the best way to become obsessed.

Now that I see it as clearly as I did that day in the gallery, I feel that somehow it has the answers I need. Ann's painted image appears to agree with me. Her smile seems to grow a little, her hand to slowly advance towards me...

Maybe because I've missed the sensation of her skin against mine, I find myself reaching too and—

Chapter Forty-One

When I open my eyes, the rush is immediate. Violent. A choir of alarmed voices surrounds me. I blink painfully, my vision unstable. Slowly, one voice detaches itself from the commotion, the syllables only beginning to make sense to my ears.

"Max! Max, are you okay?"

I try to answer. An incoherent mumble escapes my lips.

"You fainted, what happened? Can you get up?"

I feel hands under my arms, forcing me to my feet, my legs wobbling at the effort. I immediately stumble and let myself be guided towards a couch nearby. Though my vision clears up a little, I struggle to recognise my surroundings.

"I don't understand, Max," the same voice says, ringing close to my right ear. "Why are you dressed like that? Where did you even find those clothes? And when did you have time to change? We split for, like, ten minutes, maybe! Max, please answer me!"

I run a hand on my collar, the familiar material of my dress grounding me a little. The fog in my brain evaporates just enough, leaving me with one question.

"Where's Ann?" I manage to say, though not much more than a whisper.

"Ann? Who's Ann?"

"Where is she?" I insist, panic fuelling my voice.

"Max, you're not making any sense. There's no Ann here."

The finality in the person's tone is enough to snap me back to reality, my vision settling. I look around at the small group of people gathered too close, a few of them already moving away as I seem to recover. When I spot someone pointing their phone at me, barely hidden between two tall men, a sliver of truth rushes to my brain.

"What..." I try. "How am I here?"

"Oh, Max!"

I finally understand why the voice sounded so familiar when Katie jumps on me, trapping me in a hug.

"Katie? Wait, no, what's going on?"

"I don't know, I was so scared!" she cries, not letting go of me. "I was at the back of the gallery and suddenly, I heard a scream, and you were on the floor, unconscious, wearing those... those weird clothes."

"Mrs Allander and Alma worked hard to make them fit, don't be rude," I reply sharply.

"Mrs... What? Max, are you high?"

A hysterical laugh escapes my lips at her question. Which quickly turns into a wounded sob. Then a panicked cry.

I lunge to my feet and turn to the wall, relieved for a short instant to find the portrait still hanging there. Our portrait.

But.

Ann's smile has disappeared, her expression left cold and empty.

And I'm not there anymore.

I'm not on the canvas.

Ann is alone against the dark background that now seems to drown her features. There's no trace of us left.

Desperate, I reach for the painting, slapping my palms over and over against it, shouting at it to take me home, that it was a mistake, that

I didn't mean to come here. I beg it to please, *please*, take me back to Ann...

Nothing happens. The portrait stays quiet, the pull between us vanished.

Devastated with shock, with incomprehension, I drop to the floor. I barely hear Katie, who's shaking me by the shoulders, telling me to stop scaring her, to get up and come home. I repeat Ann's name over and over until the tears and the gasps make it impossible to move my lips.

All around me, I hear my own name being called in desperation, Katie's voice mixing with the one alive in my memories.

Chapter Forty-Two

"Max, I need you here... I beg you, please wake up..."

My head feels heavy when I try to open my eyes, my throat sore with the hopeless cries I can still hear ringing in my ears.

"I need to go back..." I whimper feebly.

"Max!"

A sudden weight settles on my right, my body tipping slightly towards it.

"I need to go back," I repeat, begging the person to understand, to help me.

"You aren't going anywhere, Max. Please, stay with me!"

I let out a harsh gasp at the scent that hits my nose then, the heavenly blend that always seems to linger on Ann's skin. As I reach for her blindly, relief flutters in my chest when she crowds against me, not leaving an inch between us. She covers my face with wet kisses, sniffing all the while.

"It better not be snot..." I try to joke before coughing roughly.

Ann leans away and adjusts my pillow, her hands shaking. She helps me sit up, then smooths my hair back until my cough ceases.

"Max, what in God's name happened? Janet found you fainted in her room and came to us, screaming you were dead!"

"Such a flair for the dramatic."

"It isn't the time for jest!"

I close my eyes at her anger, sorry that I'm the reason her self-control is in shreds. But she settles close to me once more, her face buried against my shoulder.

"I am sorry, Max, please forgive me. I... I have been so scared and worried. I did not know what to do. You kept calling my name, but you never woke up..."

Her hand in mine, I blink away the tears, bits of my dream coming back to me. But was it a dream? Did I actually go back to my time, even just for a moment? It all seemed so real. Katie seemed so real. But I'm here now and Ann couldn't feel more present against me. Which one did I dream? Am I dreaming now?

I pinch myself and inhale sharply at the pain. Not dreaming then. It takes me a minute longer to sort out my thoughts and memories, trying to figure out how to explain.

"You've seen the painting, right? In Janet's room?"

"The painting?" Ann repeats, frowning. "There was a sheet covering something now that I think of it, but I cannot say whether it was a painting."

"It is. It's our painting, the one that brought me here."

"How is this possible?" she exclaims. "Benedict has not finished it yet. How could it be here?"

"Because Benedict's isn't right. But Janet's is. She made the portrait of us that I've seen."

I give her a second to absorb the information.

"When did you learn this?"

"A few weeks ago," I confess, the thoughts rushing through my head coming out in a jumbled mess. "I didn't say anything about Benedict's because I was scared of the painting. I don't think I wanted it to exist. I was afraid of what could happen. And I was right because when Janet showed me hers, there was this weird pull I felt..."

I sigh, my headache making its grand return.

"I don't know what happened exactly earlier. I was going to show it to you when you came home, but I just... I don't know... There's something that—"

"Did you wish to go back?" Ann interrupts, her voice too quiet.

"No! Or... maybe? I'm not sure what I expected to happen..."

She turns her head against my shoulder, looking down at our joined hands.

"If you did wish to... go back... I would understand."

Ann glares at me when I snort.

"I don't know if I actually did travel back for a moment or if it was just in my head. But it confirmed that I meant it before, when I said I didn't want to go back."

I'm myself surprised by how easily the words come to me, as if it wasn't the most important decision I ever had to make.

"I mean, hot showers, jeans and good coffee are not enough to make me want to live in a world where people film someone struggling instead of helping," I try to joke, hoping to relieve the tension a little.

"I did not understand a word of that," Ann mutters.

I'm happy to hear a note of amusement in her voice, though it still feels unreachable to me. As I shut my eyes for a second, a glimpse of the dread I felt at being back in the future returns, but not only that. There's guilt. A strong, crushing, nasty guilt.

"I saw someone there, wherever I was, someone I didn't treat as well as she deserved."

"Oh," Ann says softly. "The person you mentioned before? Is she... Was she important to you?"

"She should have been. But I don't think I was able to give her what she needed then. It wasn't working between us, I knew it, and I acted awfully out of frustration... She deserved better."

"And... Did you think of her when you were close to our portrait? Is that why this happened?"

I let out a humourless laugh.

"Honestly, I wish I could say yes to feel less terrible, but no. Since I arrived here, I just... forgot about her. About everyone I knew. And I guess I feel pretty guilty about how much I just don't care. My previous life wasn't great, you know, but it was something I built and that was entirely mine. It shouldn't be so easy to just... discard it."

Though I hate feeling Ann tense against me, I also know that if I don't say this now, it might stay unspoken. An invisible barrier between us.

"I spent a lot of years trying to fit in, trying to find the right person for me, the right job, the right place. Everything I did was a rushed succession of events. Nothing ever felt right or enough. But I kept trying and trying."

I roll on my side, tucking my restless hands under the pillow.

"Coming here wasn't something I did or worked for, it's something that *happened* to me. And somehow, it felt right from the very beginning. It felt easy and natural, something I never had before," I say, staring at the window behind Ann's head, unable to look at her just now. "I know I said a few times I wanted to go back, but the truth is, I don't think I ever meant it. I don't think I actually liked my life before. I was alone and lonely and mostly miserable. But then, I met you. And your mother, Alma, Alice, Janet. My family. You all turned my world upside down just by making me feel like I belong. You gave me a home. I wouldn't give that up for anything in the world."

Ann smiles wetly at that. I reach for her cheek to wipe the tear falling down, feeling lighter when I see that my hands have stopped shaking.

"So I'm sorry I scared you. I didn't mean to because I love you very, very much and I don't want to leave you, ever," I say softly.

Ann lunges at me then, more gracefully than I would ever be able to. Some time passes without a word uttered between us.

"But wait," I say suddenly, emerging from our relieved kisses when I realise something. "How come you're here? Last time I was conscious, you were still gone with no news as to when you were coming back?"

"I returned as a surprise, on the day you fainted."

"Ah. And I'm assuming I ruined the surprise?"

The look she gives me is enough of an answer.

"Benedict arrived on the same evening and was out of sorts to find you in this state. I have asked Jeremiah to take him back to Squareshaw Park so that he wouldn't be left to worry on his own. Benedict almost refused to leave."

"Wait," I say, glancing at the night sky through the window and wondering how that much could have happened in just a few hours. "How long have I been out?"

"A little more than a day," Ann replies, the strain evident in her voice.

"Huh. No wonder my body feels so stiff. I guess we should tell everyone I'm awake?"

But Ann shakes her head vehemently before sliding under the sheets to join me.

"Not yet."

So I pass my arm around her to bring her close and drop a kiss on her forehead, smiling when she hums softly.

Epilogue

The following morning, Ann accepts to share the good news of my coming back to life with everyone else. But she also refuses to let me pretend I lost all my memories of them and that I'm from the future. Which is a shame; it would have been really credible.

Alma, Alice and Janet jump on me and refuse to let go until Mrs Allander asks for her turn, gentler than the horde that rushed me. Benedict repeats an exhausting amount of time how relieved he is that I'm well and with my mind intact. Even Twain seems somewhat glad to see me awake, hiding his obvious ecstasy behind a mask of indifference.

They all accept the vague explanation Ann and I provide as to why I fainted, but some days after, we learn that Janet worried she was to blame, when she publicly confesses her passion for art one evening. Far from reprimanding her, Mrs Allander encourages her to make time to hone her skills and also asks her to paint a family portrait which, yes, includes me.

Later, Ann and I debate what to do with our own painting. Even though we're all very proud of Janet—to her highest pleasure and surprise—I don't trust myself around it on a daily basis. So it's decided that Janet will keep it until we're gone, before it's moved to Alice's room at her request.

As autumn comes to term, the wedding goes ahead, despite the doubts and hesitations we all shared. It's a lovely day, especially as Alma and White are married at the same time, the two sisters sharing the altar. Mrs Allander stays dignified until the end, but I can see how much it pains her to have two of her daughters leave at once.

Directly after the ceremony, Alma and White move to his London townhouse. They promise to come for Alice in a few weeks once they're settled, so that she can enjoy all the capital has to offer. Alice answers readily that if they do not take her to the circus, she *will* run away to become a clown herself. Though confused at first, White promptly learns that humour is not to be neglected in this family.

Finding a solution that fitted the four of us was more complicated. Simply moving to London could have been an option, but Benedict and Twain were reluctant after too many years of hiding and struggling there. We brushed the possibility of moving further away where no one knew us. Ann turned it down quickly as she refused to be separated from her family, and I wasn't too keen on the idea either.

In the end, the perfect solution came up unexpectedly when a sympathetic acquaintance of the two men decided to sell his property, conveniently located north of Croydon, between London and the Allanders' house. A single visit was enough to convince us all.

Ann was charmed by the grounds and the beautiful stream crossing the surrounding woods. Always practical, Twain was pleased by the manageable size of the house, which implied less staff and more privacy. Benedict quickly pointed out a room in their wing that could be both his studio and their shared library. As for myself, I never felt quite comfortable at Squareshaw Park; it was too grand, too luxurious, too fragile. But this house made leaving the Allanders' easier. It felt warm and inviting. It felt like a home. I could already imagine our life there, happy and peaceful.

Once the arrangements confirmed, Ann and Twain leave first for our new house. Benedict and I stay behind for a few days, for appearances. The plan is then for us two to "visit" the married couple for a few weeks, then to spend some time apart in London or at the Allanders', until the wedding becomes old news. Then we'll move in indefinitely. The excuse we came up with to justify our arrangement if questions were to arise is that Benedict is going to help with Twain's responsibilities, and I'll be a companion to Ann while her husband is busy or absent. It feels shaky, yes, but we'll make it work.

So until we can join our partners, Benedict and I spend our days together with Alice and Janet, and our evenings chatting agreeably with Mrs Allander.

Though I wish we could, we all know it wouldn't be possible for her, Alice and Janet to come live with us. Not that Mrs Allander would want to, anyway. Especially now that, thanks to the new Mrs White and her husband, the house belongs entirely to her. I don't think she could bear the idea of leaving the home where her daughters grew up and where she had been so happily married. I understand it too well. A sharp sadness rushes me as I walk the corridors on the final evening, on my way to join her for a nightcap.

Both of us stay silent for a long time.

"I still recall the worry I felt on that very first day when my daughters brought home a lost, dishevelled and strangely dressed person," Mrs Allander says finally.

I can't help but smile at the memory, wondering if I had already guessed then how much I would grow to love those people.

"Sometime later, I remember wondering at how easy it had been to become accustomed to your presence with us. But I know now it was because even then, I knew you belonged with our family. You filled the gap in our hearts that my dear departed husband left."

I don't even try to answer, aware that I have lost all control of my voice. But when Mrs Allander speaks again, awkwardness takes the lead on my emotions.

"I cannot pretend to understand the... friendship between you and Ann. Nor the exact nature of your current arrangement."

She smiles at my startled expression before adding mysteriously,

"I know everything that happens in my house."

And I beg silently that she doesn't, because that would be incredibly embarrassing.

"I wanted you to know before you join Ann that I am so very glad the two of you found each other. I wish you every happiness."

One thing I respected about Mrs Allander from the start is that she was no nonsense and, like me, not a huge amateur of hugs. But if I could learn to like them, she could as well. I don't give her time to react before I wrap my arms around her neck. I hold the awkward position for a few seconds, amused to hear her stammering. Eventually, she pats my back and I take it as an accomplishment, letting go.

We say goodbye in the morning, Alice clinging to my waist, tears rolling down her cheeks. I take her aside while Benedict helps to hang our stuff on the back of the carriage. He convinced the man Twain sent to let me drive for a few miles, so that should be fun. Or possibly deadly.

Alice refuses to meet my eyes, sniffing and wiping her cheeks with the back of her sleeve. She stares resolutely at Fitz, who's circling close to her legs as if to console her. Pressing a finger under her chin, I make Alice look up at me.

"I'm not leaving forever, you know."

"I do not see the difference. Ann, Alma, and you have all abandoned me."

"I promise you we're not," I say before throwing an exaggerated look around, as if to make sure no one is listening.

That's enough to capture Alice's curiosity.

"I'm not supposed to tell you, but... We're planning to meet at Alma's in London in a few weeks when you'll be there. It's possible an unforgettable adventure awaits us."

"You promise?" she asks, sounding more eager than ever.

"I promise, kiddo. You know I can't lie to you. You're too smart for me."

Alice snorts, her usual brightness returning.

"That I am! Go now," she orders, gesturing towards the carriage. "I need to prepare for our adventure."

I am a little concerned she'll somehow get her hands on explosives or something as ridiculous, but that's a worry for another day.

As the carriage rolls down the path, I wave at Mrs Allander, Alice and Janet through the window. I watch them grow smaller in the distance, already missing the sight of the house I came to consider as my home.

Though I suppose, if I were to be incredibly sappy, I would say that Ann is my home.

My smile freezes when my eyes land on Janet. Taken by a sudden doubt, I reach under Mrs Allander's shawl, tightly wrapped around my shoulders, and pat my pocket. I sigh in relief to find it empty of the letter of recommendation I've asked of Benedict's former master some weeks ago. Janet should find it soon enough.

When we reach our new house a couple of hours later than planned, Twain shakes his head at the result of the slight incident we may have had while I was driving. Ann pats me worryingly before giving me a light slap at the back of the head for scaring her once again. I pretend to sulk by the carriage as she complains to Twain about my inconsiderate treatment of her nerves. He teases her kindlier that he would me, but I still grant him a smile at a particularly well-placed joke.

Hat in hand, Benedict bows exaggeratedly to Ann and asks for the formidable honour of escorting the new Mrs Twain inside. They go up the stairs, not bothering to wait for the rest of us. As I am left with Twain, we exchange a wary look, but I let out a sigh and give him my arm.

"Come on, Jeremiah. We shouldn't make them wait."

With a startled laugh, he accepts my extended arm, and we enter the house, guided by our partners' happy chattering.

The door closes behind us with a sense of relief. I drop Jeremiah's arm to take hold of Ann's hand, determined to never let go.

About the Author

Charlotte Rowan is a translator based in Edinburgh and now an author of queer fiction, with a passion for endless pining and characters with feelings bigger than them.

In her spare time, she can be found doodling away, wandering in ruins of Scottish castles or hunting for obscure records.

Excellent LGBTQ+ fiction by unique, wonderful authors.

Thrillers

Mystery

Romance

Young Adult

& More

Join our mailing list here for news, offers and free books!

Visit our website for more Spectrum Books

www.spectrum-books.com

Or find us on Instagram

@spectrumbookpublisher

www.ingramcontent.com/pod-product-compliance
Lightning Source LLC
Chambersburg PA
CBHW030301200626
46816CB00002BA/727